Son of the Cursed Bear

(Sons of Beasts, Book 1)

T. S. JOYCE

Son of the Cursed Bear

ISBN-13: 978-1973910350
ISBN-10: 1973910357
Copyright © 2017, T. S. Joyce
First electronic publication: July 2017

T. S. Joyce
www. tsjoyce.com

All Rights Are Reserved. No part of this book may be used or reproduced in any manner whatsoever without written permission, except in the case of brief quotations embodied in critical articles and reviews. The unauthorized reproduction or distribution of this copyrighted work is illegal. No part of this book may be scanned, uploaded or distributed via the Internet or any other means, electronic or print, without the author's permission.

NOTE FROM THE AUTHOR:

This book is a work of fiction. The names, characters, places, and incidents are products of the writer's imagination or have been used fictitiously and are not to be construed as real. Any resemblance to persons, living or dead, actual events, locale or organizations is entirely coincidental. The author does not have any control over and does not assume any responsibility for third-party websites or their content.

Published in the United States of America

First digital publication: July 2017
First print publication: July 2017

Editing: Corinne DeMaagd
Cover Photography: Wander Aguiar
Cover Model: Dylan Horsch

DEDICATION

For Asher.

ACKNOWLEDGMENTS

I couldn't write these books without some amazing people behind me. A huge thanks to Corinne DeMaagd, for helping me to polish my books, and for being an amazing and supportive friend. Looking back on our journey here, it makes me smile so big. You are an incredible teammate, C!

Thanks to Dylan Horsch, the cover model for this book and couple of my others. Any time I get the chance to work with him, I take it because he has always been good to me. Thank you to Wander Aguiar and his amazing team for this shot for the cover. You always get the perfect image for what I'm needing.

And last but never least, thank you, awesome reader. You have done more for me and my stories than I can even explain on this teeny page. You found my books, and ran with them, and every share, review, and comment makes release days so incredibly special to me.

1010 is magic and so are you.

ONE

Nox Fuller hated just about everyone, but at the top of that list were the fire breathers.

It was a new hatred, thanks to Damon Daye summoning him like some bellman to his overpriced, cold-as-a-dead-fish cliff mansion and bullying him into being here. Right here—cruising past the *Foxburg, Pennsylvania Population 183* sign. The blue dragon was a twat-muffin, and if it weren't for his threat to kick Nox out of his mountains and/or fucking *eat* him, he would've been back home, relaxing in his trailer, enjoying rare-as-a-unicorn time off right now. But no. Instead of making his way through a six pack with a few steaks sizzling on his grill, he was here in between bounty hunting jobs, tracking down Damon Daye's son, Vyr.

Fucking. Dragons.

He should just kill Vyr. His bear rumbled a growl up his throat, because even though he was a beast, he was all about survival. If he killed the red dragon, then the Son of Kong would be all mad at Nox for murdering his best friend, and the asshole gorilla shifter would probably kill him before he even Changed into his grizzly. Everyone was scared of Vyr because he was an out-of-control fire breather, a man-eater, and blah blah blah. Everyone was scared of him but Nox.

Nah, Torren was the one to watch. Vyr only shifted into his dragon once every few weeks. Torren Changed all the time like he couldn't help it. He was a fully mature silverback shifter gone years too long without a family group under him, and he was half off his rocker. He pretended he wasn't, but Nox was the son of Clinton Fuller. He could spy crazy from a mile away.

Everyone thought Nox was the insane one, but he fucking *wasn't*. He just hated everyone and didn't want to play lets-talk-about-the-weather. Reclusive didn't equal crazy. Torren and Vyr were the nut jobs.

Nox gripped the steering wheel as he coasted into the parking lot of the Foxburg Inn sitting pretty on the edge of the Allegheny River. Cute town if you were into scenic mountains and that small hometown feel. Everyone probably knew everyone here. The trees were different, the houses, and the smell of this place too, but in a way, it reminded him of home. Damon's Mountains were a lot like these, which is probably why Vyr had picked the Appalachians.

Too bad he was going to shifter prison for a year.

That's fuckin' right. Nox was here to bounty hunt his fire-breathin' ass, and he was good at his job. His phone dinged with a notification so Nox pulled to a stop to check it. Big Stupid Red Dragon just used his credit card at the local grocery store. Idiot didn't understand the first thing about being on the lam. Cash only.

Nox moved to turn his old work truck around, but stopped midway through the first rotation of the steering wheel. As a man of deep instincts, the hair rose on the back of his neck. Sure, he had two devils on his shoulders, no angels, but those devils had kept him out of trouble a hundred times. And right now, they were whispering, "the timing is weird."

It was. Vyr was a big, mindless sky lizard when he was Changed, but as a man? Vyr wasn't that dumb. This was the second time using a credit card, and it happened right as Nox rolled into town? Hell no. Was he the one being hunted?

Nox narrowed his eyes at the line of shops down the street. He already knew this town. That's what he did when he went on a hunt. He researched a place to death so there was less risk of being caught off-guard. He needed to ease into this one. Wait a minute and figure out what was going on before he charged the Red Dragon both guns a-blazin'. Or in his case, all claws out.

Nope. He wasn't going after him right now. Both devils on his shoulders nodded in unison and gave sharp-toothed smiles.

Nox parked in the inn lot, right over the line so no human fart-knuckles got the genius idea to park right next to him, ding his work truck, and bring on the wrath of Nox's bear. He lived alone deep in Damon's Mountains for a reason. As he looked up at the inn, he sighed in irritation at the thought of being crammed in there with other people. His mood was about to take a turn for the worse, and there wasn't a damn thing he could do about it but blame the beast in his middle. He was a loner bear, rogue maybe, hell if he knew. All Nox knew was people—humans and shifters alike—made him want to rampage.

New plan. He was going to check into the inn, then wait until he knew the Red Dragon would be far away from the store, and then he was going to do some recon. Maybe tomorrow, if his instincts settled down, he would bring in the Red Dragon. This was dangerous because Vyr wasn't careful. He was unpredictable, and with Torren as his bodyguard? Nox could have his throat ripped out and his carcass burned within seconds. They hated him, and the feeling was pretty fuckin' mutual. Damon Daye wanted his son brought in as quietly as possible, so it meant Nox had no back-up and he had to be even more careful than usual.

Maybe tomorrow he would be the missile that blew Vyr's fucking world out of the water.

Tonight? The devils on his shoulders were too loud. They wanted to survive Vyr's fire.

Tonight he hunted on the outskirts of the Red Dragon's new territory, and quietly.

TWO

Nevada Foxburg exhaled a long, shaky breath and tried to gather the courage to push open the door of her silver Maxima. *Just do it. There's not that many people here.*

This was the talk she had with herself every time she went grocery shopping.

Social anxiety was a B-word to deal with on a good day, but this week it had been particularly draining.

She tried again, but yanked her hand away from the door handle and then, in frustration with herself, she slammed her head back against the seat rest. *Freaking do it!*

It wasn't even the thought of going into the store

and picking out food in the nighttime hours when most women wouldn't have dreamed of shopping alone. It was the number of cars in the parking lot. There were five. Two of them belonged to the cashier, Jimmy, and the manager of the small grocery store, Esmerelda, but that left three other cars that had to be customers. It was eleven o'clock on a Tuesday, and it wasn't usually this busy. She'd systematically come at different times to figure out when was the least busy, but this Tuesday had bucked the trend. She needed peanut butter and bananas and cheese crackers and toothpaste and bread and a gallon of vanilla ice cream to deal with this week's tomfoolery. Yet here she sat, tracking the progress of two guys in work-out clothes chattering happily as they walked across the parking lot and into the store.

Why couldn't she be like them? Stores and crowds obviously bothered them zero percent.

And they were human. They didn't have an animal to call on when they were defensive. Not like her. She was the wussiest shifter that had ever been born.

Pouting out her lip, Nevada closed her eyes and counted to five, then forced herself to push open the door. Essie's Pantry was the only grocery store within thirty miles open this late, and it was closing in an hour. She needed to get this over with.

Focus on one step in front of the other. Don't be weird if someone says hi. People do that out of politeness, not rudeness. Good grief, where was her animal? Right now, she couldn't even feel it. The little critter had holed up deep inside of her, terrified as usual, curled into such a tight little ball she felt non-existent.

The car beeped when she locked it with her key. She gathered her purse close to her like a shield and made her way across the small two lanes between the parking lot and Essie's. Eyes on the sliding glass doors, she nearly jumped out of her skin when a truck locked up their brakes and skidded to a stop right next to her. Nevada lurched back and screamed in terror as the rusty, old red and silver Dodge Ram rocked to a stop.

"What the fuck, lady?" the guy behind the wheel yelled out his open window. "Watch where I'm driving!"

Nevada stood frozen in the middle of the road, trapped in the man's furious, piercing blue gaze, her thighs only inches from the front bumper of the truck. Oh, he was mean. So mean she couldn't make herself move if she tried. His beard was thick and covered the bottom half of his face, but his blond hair was cut short on the sides and grown out longer on top. He looked like a Viking. Even from here, she could see his muscular shoulders pressing against the plaid material of his shirt. His size made him even more intimidating, but it was the direct way he held her gaze that scared her the most.

"Helloooo?" he asked, waving a hand in front of his face.

No response from her. She might as well have been a popsicle right now. A terrified popsicle.

The man sighed loudly, and then it tapered into something horrifying. A loud, snarling rumble emanated from the truck as he clenched his bright white teeth around the sound. He narrowed his eyes and dragged his attention to her tits, then back up to her eyes. "Kindly, get out of the way," he gritted out.

He'd been the one who almost hit her! She was on the crosswalk and had the right of way. "You're really mean," she whispered in a shaking breath.

The man looked taken aback, and some of the

anger faded from his face. "Thank…you."

"Okay then," she murmured with a nod. He was a weird one, clearly, and she was also a weird one, and this conversation wouldn't go anywhere productive. She ducked her head and made her way into the store in quick, jerky steps at a speed walk her trainer would be proud of.

She wished she could go right back to her car, drive out of here, and survive on air for dinner, but she didn't want to give that animal the satisfaction of watching her run away like the little chicken she was. That's what she should've been—a chicken shifter. Bock, bock.

Cheeks on fire, she shook her head and tried to stop herself from replaying how awkward she'd been with that man. She always did that—went over and over how strange she was in conversations—and it never solved anything. It just made her feel bad about herself.

With trembling hands, she pulled her list out of her purse, along with a purple pen, and then made a beeline for the produce, determined to stock up on everything so she didn't have to shop for another two weeks.

She scrambled around, speed-shopping, but as she was shoving nectarines into a plastic bag, a low catcall whistle sounded. Mortified, she looked up, expecting it to be the strange man who had almost squashed her on the pavement like a bug under a boot. It wasn't, though. It was one of the guys in the workout clothes she'd seen earlier. The dark-haired one was nodding and looking at her like she was a piece of steak, and the other was staring directly at her tits with a gross, predatory smile that gave her chills across her forearms. Great. The exact kind of attention she hated. She didn't recognize them, and the town was basically a village. She'd grown up in Foxburg and knew everyone. These guys were probably tourists.

She jerked her attention away from them and scurried to the next aisle. So she was a few nectarines short—better to be safe than sorry. An older man was there, staring at the frozen vegetables behind the glass freezer doors. When he looked at her and offered a friendly smile, she fought the urge to turn around and find somewhere unoccupied.

"Good evening," he said, shoving his glasses farther up his nose.

"I'm fine, thank you." *Oh my gosh, what was that?* Embarrassed, she grabbed a loaf of bread and plopped it in her basket without even checking the expiration date.

Motoring her legs, she booked it to the Pop Tarts, but those guys were there. She skidded to a stop at the entrance and backed out slowly. Only the guys followed, casting each other glances, laughing. Messing with her. Jerks.

She whipped the cart around and made her way to the back. Milk and eggs. And some oxygen because she couldn't breathe right now. Her chest was so tight she was on the verge of panicking. She'd done that before too, walked out of a store and left all her groceries in the basket just because she couldn't handle the crowd.

"What's your name?" the dark-haired guy asked.

Chills, chills, chills everywhere, and this wasn't just social anxiety anymore. Her inner fox had woken up and was growling. There was something wrong with these men. They prickled her instincts and made her want to run, or fight, or maybe both.

Fast as she could, Nevada yanked a gallon of one-percent milk from the fridge and then shoved her cart toward the eggs.

"Come on, don't play hard to get. I'm only asking your name." He was moving toward her slowly, flanked by his friend.

Can't breathe.

Freak the eggs, she couldn't stay here. Nevada pushed her cart around a fridge full of bacon and slice-and-bake cookies. But when she tried to maneuver into a new aisle, the dark-haired man was there, hands out in placation, an empty smile on his face.

"It was just a question, and you're running like I'm after you. Chill. I'm just talking."

Nevada was trapped between the center aisle fridges unless she backed up, but when she went to turn her cart, the other guy was behind her with a feral smile. When the dark-haired man approached, she abandoned the cart, ready to jump over one of the fridges to get away from them. The other guy was closing in, and she really couldn't draw a breath into her lungs right now. Tears burned her eyes. Weak. She had a knife in her purse. Why would a shifter ever have to carry a knife when they had teeth and claws? Because her animal was no help. Never had been. She might as well have been human.

She fumbled for the knife, but it wasn't in the pocket where she usually kept it, and both of them were too close. Too close!

Her butt hit the fridge as she looked back and forth between the two men.

"Fuckwit number one and fuckwit number two, back away from the lady before I remove your heads."

Nevada jerked her gaze to the bearded man from the parking lot, leaning on the other side of the fridge like he'd been there all along. His voice had come out completely calm, but his eyes were an inhuman silver color, and his face was twisted into something terrifying.

"Fuck off, *shifter*," the dark-haired one said. "We're just talking to her."

Giant Weirdo with a Beardo gave an empty smile and scratched his jaw with his thumbnail. The chuckle that emanated from him was downright scary. It knocked around in her head, and the heaviness wafting from the man clogged Nevada's lungs. *Can't. Breathe!* Oh, this man was a monster, and these humans didn't have the instincts she did.

They should run. She should run. No one should be in the same building with him.

There was a loaded moment, and then the dark-haired man let off a laugh and waved his hand. "This isn't that serious." He backed away and jerked his chin at his friend. "See ya around, pretty girl," he said. His eyes were empty when he cast her a long glance over his shoulder.

"Th-thank you," she whispered.

"Save your thank yous for someone who wants them. I ain't nobody's hero. Those douche-pickles were blocking my path to the bacon. So are you. Vamoose." The bearded man waved his hand impatiently at her.

She stood there shocked, up until the point where he strode past her, carefully stepping over her sneakers and lifting his hands as though he didn't want to touch her grotesque skin.

And then he grabbed six packages of bacon, cradled them in his arm like a baby, and strode off toward the checkout counters up front, dried mud trailing behind him from where he stomped it off his dirty boots.

Alrighty then. He was possibly the rudest man

she'd ever met. But he'd just saved her, kind of. He was built like a tank. His longer hair up top was shaved into a laid-down mohawk, and tattoos peeked out from under his plaid shirt at the back of his thick neck. He walked with the confident grace of a man who knew his exact place in the world—at the top of the food chain.

Big cat, bear, gorilla, or boar shifter—those were her guesses. Well...probably not boar because it would be weird, him eating copious amounts of bacon. But maybe.

When he disappeared around the corner, she finally, finally dragged in a full breath. Chest heaving, she shopped as fast as possible and left off the last three things on her list just to get out of there. As she checked out, talking to Jimmy wasn't so bad because she knew him and he was always friendly and understanding if she said something awkward. After she paid in cash, with shaking hands, she bolted from the store. Nevada shoved her basket through the sliding doors and out to the dimly lit parking lot like cart racing was an Olympic sport. But when she got halfway to her car, the hairs lifted on her neck again. It was too quiet, and she felt watched.

She looked around, but the only person she saw was Weirdo with a Beardo sitting in his truck, one row away under the street lamp. His eyes blazed silver, and his lip was split. Red trickled down his beard, staining it, and that wasn't the only crimson on him. His hand rested on the top of the steering wheel, and his knuckles were all cut and red.

What the heck?

As she pushed the cart faster, his eyes arced across the parking lot, tracking her. This man was certifiable, and downright terrifying. She ripped her gaze away from him. A second longer trapped in it, and she was going to have a full-blown freak-out.

Panicking, she shoved her groceries in the back seat of her Maxima, spilling them everywhere, but she didn't care. She just wanted to get out of here, lock herself in her apartment, and feel okay again.

She thought about calling the police on the bleeding man in the truck as she backed out of the parking spot, but that's when movement caught her eye. She slammed on her brakes and lurched to a stop. Right on the other side of her parking space, the two men from inside were lying on the asphalt. The dark-haired one was gripping his stomach, the other was unconscious, and both their faces looked like hamburger.

Mind racing, Nevada tried to make sense of why they were by her car and not their own, two rows over.

She jerked her attention to the rearview mirror, and the bearded man was still there in his truck, eyes locked on hers through the reflective glass. He didn't look as terrifying though, not now that it was starting to make sense. Those guys had come out to the parking lot and had been waiting by her car. Why? She didn't even want to think of why. They weren't here with good intentions, though.

The rude man had taken care of them. Again.

He spat red out of the window and whipped out of his parking spot, then drove like a bat out of hell to the main road. His engine roared as he gassed it away from Essie's Pantry and disappeared into the night.

He might not want to be considered a hero...but to Nevada?

That wild and infinitely rude man had just done something very heroic.

THREE

He probably didn't like oatmeal raisin.

He probably didn't like anything.

Crap. But oatmeal raisin was the best cookies Nevada knew how to bake. She took three steps in the direction of the Foxburg Inn, but then did an about-face and marched back to her Maxima. Maybe she should've gotten him a gift card to a coffee shop as a thank you for smashing those predators' faces in for her last night. Or a handmade thank you card? She knew how to make paper. Crap, crap, crap.

She tried to inhale deeply, but her lungs always froze up on her when she was thinking about going into a building with a lot of people in it. The cookies would be fine. She'd spent all morning making them, and they tasted really good. He would probably like the cookies. Dad always told her the way to a man's heart was through his stomach. Not that she was trying to win Weirdo with a Beardo's heart, but just the same. She'd made the right decision with the cookies.

What if he wasn't at the inn, though? And how would she track down his room number? She didn't even know his first name. Maybe he wasn't staying in town at all. Maybe he'd just been passing through last night and needed to stop for bacon.

Chewing her bottom lip, Nevada looked up at the cream-colored hotel, then blew a strand of hair out of her face and forced her legs to move toward the front door. If he wasn't in there, okay, but at least she could say she tried. If she didn't try, she would always wonder what-if.

Maybe he wouldn't be there, and then she didn't have to worry about talking to him. They were both obviously bad at conversing, but she'd been taught manners, and she felt obligated to say thank you in a meaningful, oatmeal-and-raisins type of way. It definitely wasn't because he was rough, gruff, and didn't seem to care about anything, nor because he had a sexy beard, which she hadn't ever thought would be sexy before now. He looked like a lumberjack, all dressed in plaid with those big…sexy…muscles. And tattoos. Maybe he was covered in ink. She'd never been into bad boys, but then again, it wasn't like anyone was knocking on the door to her Poontang Temple, so maybe she needed to cast her net out a little wider and consider bad boys and— *Oh my gosh! No. This was a thank you, not a booty call. Focus.*

She reached for the door, chickened out twice, then succeeded on the third try. Poontang was a gross word. Where had that come from? It was as close to a curse word as she said. Mom had raised her a lady and had beaten it into her head that ladies didn't say words like that. Her mom would poop a literal brick if she knew Nevada had even thought the distasteful word.

Beardo had used the F word three times last night. She'd counted. He was bad.

And what did it say about her that she'd thought about his piercing blue eyes all night, or the way he'd felt all warm and dominant when he'd walked close to her, or the way he'd cradled that bacon like a little baby?

"Can I help you?" the woman at the front desk asked. Her name was Anita, even if it didn't say it on a nametag. Nevada knew who she was, because she'd gone to school with her. Anita had been a senior when she was a freshman in high school. She'd escaped this place for a little while, and made a life in Atlanta, but ended up right back here. Everyone did. This place was like a sinkhole.

"H-hi. Ummm." Think. "I'm looking for someone?"

"We don't give out names here. It's against policy."

"Oh, that's okay, I don't even know his name."

Anita's dark eyebrows drew down. "Okaaay."

"Um…he is about yay tall." Nevada held her hand up a foot above her head. "And he has this epic beard. Muscles. Tattoos." Her voice was going dreamy. *Cut it out!* Nevada cleared her throat and shuffled her feet nervously. "I baked him cookies. He kind of…saved me. My life. He saved my life maybe. I think. I'm not sure because I'm a little confused about how everything—"

"Don't need your life story," Anita muttered as she typed away on the computer. She hadn't been that nice in high school either.

"R-right. Do you know what room number he is staying in?"

"I already told you it's against policy to give out information." Anita's voice sounded so bored right now.

"Okay," Nevada whispered. "Sorry. Thanks anyway." She turned to leave but forced herself back around. "It's just...I really wanted to tell him thank you."

Anita rolled her head back on her shoulders, stared at the ceiling, and blew out a long, annoyed noise. And then leveled Nevada with narrowed eyes. "The description you gave..." she said slowly. "He's probably the type of man who likes to shoot whiskey."

Nevada frowned. "I beg your pardon?"

"He probably likes whiskey." Anita jerked her head to the right. "Drinking. Drinks. He probably likes drinks."

Baffled, Nevada stared at the riddle-filled woman.

"Oh, for chrissakes, he's at the bar."

Nevada jerked her attention to a small bar area on the other side of the sprawling great room. Sure enough, Beardo was there, and his icy blue eyes were trained right on her. Oooh, she wanted to run. Talking to Anita had been hard enough, but now she felt stupid and embarrassed. Heat was already creeping up her neck, and no doubt she would have cherry-red cheeks by the time she made it over to him.

And just as she'd convinced herself she should leave, Beardo shook his head in agitation and waved her over. Well, she really didn't want to do this now if he was just going to be angry with her.

As she meandered over to him, he tossed back another shot of what really did look like whiskey, and then he set the tiny glass down too hard. It made a *thunk* sound that prickled her oversensitive ears and made her jump. He was too rough. And as she got close enough, she noticed his boots were muddy. Again. He had trailed the dried chunks of it all over the carpet. This guy was a mess. A hot, sexy mess.

"I came to say thank you," she blurted out at the same time he asked, "What the fuck are you doing here?"

"Oh." Nevada laughed nervously and couldn't meet his eyes, which were staring directly and rudely right at her. She held the tin of cookies against her stomach as if that could stop the nervous flutters there.

"It ain't Christmas yet," he said in a deep, rumbling voice.

"I'm sorry?"

"What does that mean, you're sorry? Sorry for what?"

"Oh, no, it just means what?"

His blond brows jacked up like two McDonalds arches. "Then why don't you just say what?" He jammed a finger at the tin of cookies. "It's got dolphins in Santa hats. It ain't Christmas, so why are you carrying that around?"

"Oh! Right." She gave another nervous laugh and shook her head at her stupidity. "Um, this is the only tin I have. I got it from this flea market for seventy-five cents. Actually, the lady who sold it to me had the whole set, but for some reason I just wanted this one. The others had wolverines and koalas and goldfish in little Santa hats and…" He was staring at her like she'd lost her mind so she explained, "I ramble when I'm nervous. And I don't talk to a lot of people, so I'm kind of…bad…at this."

The man gave a slow blink.

Nevada shoved the tin at him, eyes averted to the carpet again. "I made these because I think you beat up those guys because they were waiting for me outside Essie's Pantry last night and my mom always told me the best way to thank someone is with an expensive gift but I can't afford expensive stuff, and furthermore I'm pretty sure she just said that because she likes when my dad buys her sparkly things and I made oatmeal raisin, but you probably don't even like that kind, but I make these best." Nevada bit her bottom lip so she would stop rambling.

"I hate cookies."

"Ha!" she blurted out, then clapped her hand over her mouth when her laugh echoed through the room. Her cheeks were on fire all the way to the tips of her ears.

"My hatred for cookies is funny?"

"Yes. No!" Nevada scrunched up her face. "A little? It's just I called it when I was going over in my head how this conversation would go. Although…" She looked around to see if people were watching, but they weren't. "It's actually going worse than I imagined. And that hardly ever happens. Usually I think of the worst-case scenario, and then when it's not so bad, I'm relieved."

Beardo's frown deepened. "So you set your expectations so low you're never disappointed."

"Well...it sounds kind of awful when you say it like that...but...yes." She shook the cookies gently to remind him to take them.

"I also have very low expectations." He yanked the tin from her hand and popped the top, then sniffed at it. "I'm going to eat all of these."

"Okay." They stared at each other for the count of three blinks, and this was her cue to leave. "Okay, thanks, bye." Nevada spun on her heel and speed walked toward the door.

"Nox."

"I'm sorry?" she asked, then shook her head and got embarrassed again. "I mean...what?"

"My name is Nox. I hate people and will be a really shitty conversationalist. I like the quiet, and I don't like new things or change. Or fuck-faces who wait in parking lots for girls."

"Okay," she said in a high-pitched voice.

"That's as close to an invite as you're going to get." He tipped his head toward the barstool beside him. And then he turned around and ordered two more shots of Jameson.

Righty-oh. She tiptoed to the chair beside him like a super-normal person and then sat down gently. The chair was leather and made a fart sound.

Nox didn't laugh, but when he looked at her, she almost saw a smile on his lips. It was riiiiight there, right at the corners.

"That wasn't what it sounded like," she uttered, mortified.

Nox leaned over, his nostrils flaring as he sniffed her. She didn't know whether to run, slap him for thinking she really farted the first thirty seconds of real time spent with him, or barf because this was the most humiliating moment of her life.

"What are you?" he asked as the bartender set the pair of shots between them, right on top of an unfolded map of Foxburg and the surrounding mountains.

"A person," she gritted out.

"Wrong answer. A, it's a boldface lie. I can hear it in your voice. Two, your eyes were bright fuckin' gold last night when those idiots had you pinned in the grocery store, and C, you smell like fur. That rules out hedgehog, sea creature, and flight shifter."

"Wait, are there sea creatures? Like…are there octopus shifters just swimming around, holding their breath and then turning back into humans? Or are you talking about mermaids? That would be really cool if there were mermaids."

Nox's eyes narrowed to crystal blue slits. "You talk a lot."

Well, that took her back. "No, I don't actually. I ramble sometimes, but mostly I'm quiet." Why was she a blabbermouth around him?

"No to mermaids and octopussies—"

"I don't think that's the plural for Octopuses. Octopi?"

"Not a bear because you're submissive as fuck, and even the most submissive bears in Damon's mountains feel way heavier than you."

Nevada flinched and gasped. "You're from Damon's Mountains?"

A soft rumbling sound emanated from him, and Nox handed her a shot. "Drink."

She stared down at the fragrant liquor in the small glass. "It's just…I'm not a very good drinker and I tend to—"

"Drink."

"Okay." Nevada jumped slightly when he tinked his glass against hers, and then she did what he did, bumped the bottom of the shot glass on the shiny bar top before she held her nose and drank the liquor down. It was gross, and it felt like she'd swallowed one of those hot pokers Dad used to stir up the fire in their fancy grand hearth in her childhood home. "I touched a hot poker once," she choked out. She showed him the pink scar across the inside of her thumb.

"So, brains aren't your gig then," Nox said rudely.

"Oh, and you never did anything silly when you were a kid?"

"Never." His voice rang with false notes though, and he smiled like he didn't even care that he was obviously fibbing. "What's your name? In my head, I've been calling you Helpless Heather."

What a jerk. "Well I've been calling you Weirdo with a Beardo." She swallowed down a gasp at her rudeness.

Nox bellowed a single, echoing laugh, just like she'd done earlier, and people turned to stare at them. Not good. Nevada shook her leg in quick succession and plucked at a loose thread on her cardigan. Today was cold, and it would snow soon, so she'd dressed in her warmest fleece leggings, knee-high boots, a red tank top and the thick gray cardigan that trailed down below her backside.

"Nevada."

"Is a pretty state," Nox muttered, giving a two-fingered wave to the bartender for more shots.

"No. I mean, yes, it is. But Nevada is my name. Nevada Foxburg."

"You're named after the town?" Nox asked, arcing a questioning gaze to her. His eyes were a pretty color of blue. Like the ocean. But not on a bad beach where the water was murky. His eyes were like the Hawaii ocean.

"Actually, the town is kind of named after me. Or not me, but my family. We've been here for generations." She shrugged up one shoulder. "We never leave."

"Hmm." The noise came out a soft rumble. "Interesting."

"I don't really like whiskey," she whispered as the bartender set down another pair of drinks in front of them.

"No shit," Nox whispered back, pushing her shot closer to her. "I could tell from the awful face you made when you took the last one. You *drank* that one. You need to *shoot* this one."

"There's a difference?"

"Yep. Open that throat up and gulp it."

"It's too much to take."

"Woman, half the shit you say I want to turn into something perverted. It's not too much for you, Nevada Foxburg." His grin turned wicked. "I know you can take all of it."

He was talking about a dick. Right? This was a dick joke? Or…flirting? She couldn't tell. This guy kept her on her toes and confused, but she kind of liked it. She kind of liked not knowing where the conversation would go with him.

She took the shot with him and felt four percent proud of herself for at least drinking it faster than last time. All Nox said was, "Needs improvement," before he ordered a plate of loaded nachos. "We're sharing," he announced gruffly.

"Oh, no thank you. I'm watching what I eat."

Nox dragged his gaze down her body, then back up to her eyes. "Whyyyy?" he drawled.

"Well, because…" Was he messing with her? She was fifty pounds overweight, and he was some kind of bodybuilder shifter. "Well, isn't it obvious?"

"You have a grabbable ass, perfect ten tits, and an hourglass shape. And I see those sexy calves under those boots. You're totally fuckable. I'd let you ride me any day, nachos or no. Besides, this place is highfalutin. It's probably non-seasoned, oven-baked pita chips and goat cheese, or some such bullshittery."

A tiny helpless sound escaped her lips. "Did you just call me fff…"

"Fuckable? Yes, I did. Look in the mirror every once in a while, woman. We're sharing nachos because no one wants a date who takes a sip of water and claims to be full. Lose weight if you want, I don't care. But to me? You look hot. I'd stick it in you."

"You say the crudest things. But that's also somehow the nicest thing anyone has ever said to me."

"Yeah? That's pretty fuckin' sad."

"You say the F-word a lot."

"It's my favorite fuckin' word in the entire fuckin' world."

"I don't cuss."

"Maybe you should. It makes everything feel better."

"Everything like what?"

Nox ripped his gaze away from her and gave it to the map under his hands. His voice was empty when he muttered, "Like life. The *F-word* makes life feel better."

"I want a puppy."

"I'm sorry," he deadpanned without looking up.

"The one I want is really cute. You wanna see a picture?"

"No. If you were a dragon and lived in these mountains," he said, jamming a finger at the map, "where would you set up your lair?"

"A real dragon?" she asked, panicking at the thought.

"Nope. Hypothetically speaking. I like to play games. If you were a dragon, and not a submissive, albeit sexy little *fox* shifter, where would you set up camp?"

Nevada nearly choked on air, and in a rush, scanned the room to see if anyone had heard. "You can't say that out loud. No one here knows."

"That you're sexy? Trust me, they know."

"No!" she whisper-screamed. "That I'm a fox."

"Yeah, I didn't think foxes existed anymore," he said at normal conversational volume.

She wanted to throat-punch him, which was insane because her tendencies were anything but violent. "I'm leaving."

"Fine." He gave her an empty look that dared her to go.

She stood and gathered her purse close. "I don't understand you."

"No one does."

"You're mean with almost everything you say, but you have these moments of goodness that keep me thinking about you."

"I'm not one of those men you'll ever fix, so if that's in your head? Leave right now. I won't change. I'm a stone. I'm not capable."

There was something so frustrating about his outright refusal to ever compromise, but there was something so intriguing about his complete honesty. Frustrating and intriguing, just enough to make her second-guess her decision to go.

"So you'll make everyone around you

compromise, and you'll never change."

Something akin to hurt flashed across his eyes, but then they went hard and cold so fast she thought she must've imagined it.

"Pretty much. I told you I don't like people, and I don't like change. Sit and eat nachos with me and talk about theoretical dragons and shoot whiskey. That's what I can offer you. Nothing more."

"Why?"

"Enough questions."

"Why can't you offer more?" she asked again, refusing to let him get out of this one. "Why can't you be nice? Why do you pick? Why when I say I don't cuss does it make you want to string them together?" *Why are you so damaged?* That last one she kept carefully in her throat, refused to let it escape because it was too deep, too soon.

His lip twitched up into a snarl. He leaned toward her. "Because I'm the son of the cursed bear, raised by beasts, raised to be affected by no one, and to lift two middle fingers to anyone who would dare try to change me. I am who I am. Accept it or leave."

"But I'm supposed to change to be more comfortable around you."

"No, Nevada Foxburg. I wouldn't ask you to change either. That's the beauty of spending an afternoon with someone who cares for nothing. You can be just who you are around me, and I won't judge."

"Because you don't care."

Nox lifted one shoulder in a shrug.

She should go. Nox was dangerous. Not only was he physically dangerous to a smaller shifter like her, but he felt dangerous to her heart too. The cursed bear? Oh, she knew who he was now. He was the only son of Clinton Fuller of the Boarlanders—half-feral, giant grizzly shifter with a wild streak so wide it had clearly stretched to his son. Nox was a grizzly. Of course, he was. But Nox was also too interesting for his own good or hers, and her every instinct screamed that he was trouble. Sexy, sexy trouble. They were doomed as friends, much less more than that. Foxes bred foxes. Thems were the rules. Even if Nox was interested, they were from two totally different worlds.

He was dangerous and safe all at once.

Slowly, she slid back onto the bar stool. And soft as a breath, she whispered, "You said I was interesting, but I think you might be the interesting one."

"Compliments will get you nowhere with me."

Nevada blew out a frustrated breath, lifting the strand of hair that had fallen in front of her face. "You're rude, uncompromising, probably don't take direction very well, and you should really clean your boots off before you walk into a place. You're too loud, too careless, and too rough, and I think someday you'll be mated only to the idea that you're better off alone because people are too much work instead of admitting it's you who caused your own loneliness."

Nox offered her a slow and genuine smile. "Much better." He nodded magnanimously. "And thank you."

FOUR

Nox was trying not to stare at Nevada.

He was trying to be a cool-boy, but she was making it so damn difficult.

Sexy. Curvy. Fox.

She was tipsy now, relaxed. He'd needed her to relax. Something was wrong with her, but he couldn't figure out if it was a problem with her human side or her animal side. She didn't like people. No. That wasn't it. She couldn't deal with people. She shrank when anyone passed too close to her chair at the bar. Even three shots in, talking to the bartender made her stutter and blush and lower her voice like she had no dominance at all. She made no sense and made all the sense in the world at once.

Why? Because Nox was fucked up around people too, just in a different way. His was an animal problem, and a self-indulgent part of him hoped her issue with her anxiety was an animal problem too, so he didn't have to feel so fucking alone with his issues.

Selfish monster. He should leave her alone.

All he did was make the people around him miserable. Oh, he knew it. He wasn't blind. Anyone he liked, he fought. Anyone he respected, he fought. Anyone he wanted to be friends with? He acted out in a way they didn't understand, and they ran or pushed him away.

And here was this woman. Fucking beautiful. Curves making her look like the number eight, grade-A tits that would fill his hands, narrow waist, thick ass. He couldn't stop thinking about bucking into her from behind. Long brown hair curled into waves, soft brown eyes that turned gold when she was scared or when someone got too close to her, full lips that gave him easy smiles the more shots she had. Red. She'd painted her lips red to match that skin-tight tank top she wore under the gray, knee-length cardigan. She was a stunner. Nothing else in here was pretty to look at but her, and it made it hard to concentrate. She kept ducking her gaze and blushing when she spoke in that soft, shy voice of hers. She was a good girl that he wanted to turn bad, and fuck what that said about him.

A short, bald dude passed too close again, and Nevada shrank away, her tits brushing the counter in her hurry to get as far away from him as possible. Nox clenched his fists on his thighs to resist the urge to rip the guy's throat out just for scaring her. Nevada was going to murder Nox's instincts if she didn't get ahold of her anxiety. Already he had shoved two guys away who had passed too close.

She was pouring over the map and nibbling on a fancy-as-fuck nacho. Her bottom lip was pouted out in concentration, and he wanted to duck under her face and suck on it. The monster in him really wanted to wipe the shot glasses and napkin dispenser off the counter, shove her on top of it, rip her pants down, and fucking unleash on her from behind. And screw whoever watched him claim her. But she wasn't corrupt like him. She probably wouldn't appreciate getting publicly dominated. But maybe? She had made him cookies. Cookies were a good sign. She'd thought about him enough to get up early and bake.

She'd spent time on these.

He opened the tin and shoved a whole cookie in his maw. Fucking delicious. He'd been a lying little liar when he'd told her he hated cookies. His sweet tooth was his favorite tooth.

"I don't remember there being any trailer parks in any of these areas," she murmured, arching her petal pink nail over a set of mountains on the map. The only one I know of is here, right outside of town."

"Huh," he murmured around the bite of cookie. Vyr and Torren wouldn't settle that close to town. The Red Dragon needed space for when he had to Change, and Torren was a bigass dominant silverback with no family group. He would need seclusion or he would go nuts. Maybe they had dragged trailers onto flat land in the mountains somewhere, but he'd done a record check and Vyr hadn't purchased land here. No one had in the last three months.

Nox scratched at the edge of his thumbnail with his pointer finger in a nervous habit he'd kept since he was a child. Maybe the Red Dragon's credit card was stolen. Or maybe Vyr was paying some asshole to make a purchase every once in a while to keep trackers off his trail. Maybe he was across the world in hiding and Nox had been duped. Perhaps he and Torren weren't here in Foxburg at all.

He'd done research on every shifter in the area, and to his knowledge, there had only been two. An old rogue grizzly up in the mountains and a female tiger shifter who only lived here in the warm months and traveled for work when the snow hit. Nox glanced out the massive picture window at the front of the room to the river outside. The clouds were gray and swirling, and the wind was whipping at the trees across the water. Snow was close, and that tiger was probably already long gone.

"Why aren't you registered?" Nox asked curiously. Usually he didn't give a shit about anyone's background, but this had been bothering him. He hadn't known fox shifters were even still around.

"Because none of us are. It's against the rules." Was that a slight slur in her pretty bell-tone voice?

He grabbed the bartender's attention with a two-fingered wave and growled out, "Water." He didn't thank the lanky man, Alex, his nametag read, when he set the drink down in front of him. Nox felt zero guilt for rudeness. He would give him a big tip instead of forcing himself to be fake-polite. Money spoke louder than words always.

"What rules?" Nox asked, pushing the ice water toward her.

She picked it up and automatically sipped it. He didn't like that. She didn't know him, and he could've roofied that drink for all she knew. He was going to have to train Nevada to be more careful when she was drinking.

"Fox rules," she whispered. "There's lots of them."

"But you're supposed to register. It's human law. They like to keep track of us."

"F-word human law."

Apparently, she really didn't cuss. For a moment, he considered saying something to piss her off to see if he could get her to say "fuck you." Barely resisting the urge, he asked instead, "How do you avoid registration? How do you avoid anyone knowing about you?"

Nevada snorted. "Step one, stay a hundred miles away from the dragons. The stupidest thing you shifters do is put yourself under their wings. You know they're targets, right? They're like this big beacon of light for human law. They're watched closely, and so are all the shifters who gather under them for protection. No one cares about foxes in Foxburg, Nox Fuller, you wanna know why?"

"Kind of," he admitted through a scowl. Why the fuck did he care about this so much?

"Because everyone's looking at Damon's Mountains, Harper's Mountains, and Kane's Mountains. They're looking at the dragons, because they're like missiles. They're the only weapons the humans are afraid of. What are a few shifters in a tiny town? Nothing to concern themselves with when they have dragons gathering armies."

"Armies?"

"Not literal armies. They're just gathering shifters in crews. Safety in numbers and all, but look at it from the humans' point of view. You have freaking dragons gathering allegiant shifters under them. Big predator shifters. Doesn't matter that they are just building families and crews and bonds and friendships. To humans? They're armies. It's easier than you'd think for lesser shifters like me to get away from registration when there are firebreathers wreaking havoc. Foxburg is safe because there are no dragons here."

Oh, the irony. Because if Nox was right, the

biggest, baddest, most volatile dragon was here somewhere. At the first sign of a fight, Vyr would burn this place to the ground and devour the ashes of Foxburg.

"That's a good theory," he said nonchalantly.

"It's not a theory. It's worked for decades for the den."

"The den?"

"The fox den. I shouldn't be talking about this." She sipped her drink again. "It's just I don't talk much at all, and sometimes I miss the sound of talking?" Nevada said it like a question, and Nox frowned.

"Why don't you hear talking?"

"Because I'm on the outside of the den. Always on the outside. I'm different, and different for foxes is a very bad thing. I'm not shunned, but people don't seek me out either. I work from home because I'm scared of people. I play music all the time or I would drown in silence. And lately I talk to myself because I miss the sound of a voice."

"Is that why you were shopping late last night?"

She dipped her chin once and wouldn't meet his gaze. Shame tinted her cheeks red. "I have brothers and sisters. Lots of them. We make big families. Have lots of kits. They all found pairs, and my parents can't find a match for me, so I just stay the same, year after year, no improvement, stagnant, living in a town where I don't belong."

"Your parents make a match for you? That's fucked up."

"It's not…effed up…if you're like me and can't find a match on your own. Who is gonna deal with all of this mess?" she asked, swirling her finger at herself. "I can't even shop during the day. Can't talk to people."

"You're talking to me just fine."

"You're different, and I'm tipsy."

Well, that actually made him feel pretty good. She'd called him *different*. He was okay with being different. But as she sipped her water and dared a look directly at him with those pretty, soft brown eyes, he was struck by the moment. He could see her future stretched depressingly in front of her. He imagined her in this loveless match with some faceless fox shifter who would keep her stagnant forever. Nox wanted to kill her future mate, and he didn't even know him.

When a snarl escaped his chest, Nevada flinched and dropped her gaze. "Sorry," she whispered.

"It ain't you. Best you don't talk about your parents making matches anymore. My shifter culture doesn't like that." He needed an out before he blabbed about how protective of her he felt. She'd told him any pairing outside of the fox shifter culture would be doomed. Like a damn Romeo and Juliet kind of doomed. That, and he wasn't made to pair up, so even that thought was terrifying. She shouldn't be on his radar, but here he was imagining ten different ways to fuck her and make her not see anyone but him. He was the real missile, aimed straight for her, and she didn't even realize how much destruction he could cause. He needed to walk away, forget about her, bounty hunt the shit out of Vyr, get him thrown in shifter prison, then blow this Popsicle stand like he did every other town he hunted in. It was safest for him, but somehow, more importantly, it would be safest for Nevada, too. She was unregistered? She sure as hell didn't need Vyr here drawing human attention. And he would. He was the least careful dragon in existence. He gave zero fucks about burning property, and he was a loud and proud man-eater.

Nox had a job to do. Get Vyr the hell out of here,

forget Nevada and her fucked-up matchmaking fox den, and go back home to his trailer and solitary life deep in Damon's Mountains where a loner like him belonged.

"Gotta go. Your cookies weren't horrible," he muttered, throwing down a few twenties for the drinks and nachos and a good tip.

He was about to walk away when he grabbed the tin of baked goods, and for a split second, he only wanted it for the excuse to track her down and return it when the cookies were gone. He'd already put a tracker on her car at the grocery store. He didn't even know why he'd done it. He'd just wanted the option of seeing her again. Bad Nox.

In a rush, he set the container on the bar top and strode away without looking at Nevada. He tossed her a two-fingered wave over his shoulder though, which was more of a goodbye than he gave most people.

"Do you want to come to a family dinner with me?" Nevada blurted out behind him.

Well, that stopped him in his tracks. He must've heard her wrong. Slowly, he turned. "You want me to come meet your parents?" Hell must've frozen over.

No one had ever invited him to meet the parents.

Nevada looked like a frightened rabbit. "It's just…"

Her voice was soft as a breeze and even Nox, with his oversensitive hearing, could barely hear her. He took a few steps closer. "It's just what?"

"It's just I'm the black sheep of my family, and I hate going to these things. We could just go as friends, but if people say mean things, you would tell them to F off. But you would say the whole word."

"What whole word?" he asked innocently. *Say it!*

"F-U-C-K," she spelled out. Damn. Clever fox.

"Why are they mean to you?"

Nevada dipped her gaze to his boots and frowned the cutest fucking little frown he'd ever seen. "I think because I'm different. Different isn't good for us. They don't like that I can't talk to people easily. And everyone else is tough, so I'm easy to pick on."

She was asking for help. For him to act as a buffer. He gave a glance to the door and sighed. He should've run sooner. "If I say yes, it's just because I like to fight and your dinner sounds like maximum drama."

"The maxim…est."

"And also free food."

"Fancy free food. The special on the menu is sea bass this week."

"It's not because I like you, or care at all, or give a shit about protecting you," he lied.

Nevada nodded, and her eyes got round like twin moons. "Okay."

"I want more cookies as payment."

"Deal."

"And a BJ."

Nevada's cheeks went cherry red, and she tucked her chin to her chest.

Time for another lie. "That was a joke."

"Oh. Right," she said with a forced laugh. "I knew that."

Spending more time with her was a bad idea. Unfortunately, Nox was a super-fan of bad ideas. "When is the dinner?"

"Tomorrow night. H-here-here's the address," she stammered as she rifled through her little purse. With shaking hands, she held out a business card.

Nox strode back toward her and yanked it out of her fingers as rudely as he could so she wouldn't fall in love with him. "Foxburg Country Club," he read aloud. He laughed. "A country club? Woman, have you seen this?" He circled a finger around his bearded face and then pulled up the shoulder of his favorite plaid shirt. "This fine specimen of a man was not made for country clubs."

"You'll be the most interesting person there." Nevada's eyes were on the ground again, and goddamn, he wished he could have seen her face better when she'd uttered that.

"Okay. What time?"

"Really?" she said too loud. "I mean…six o'clock. Wear whatever you want."

Nox snorted. "Okay, I'll probably be wearing this for the third day in a row." She didn't look nearly disturbed enough so he threw in, "And also cut-off short shorts. I'm not shaving my legs either. You're welcome."

"Great. Great, that's great. I'll wear something to match you."

Well, that was a surprising answer. "Matching is for losers."

She parted her lips to say more, but Nox turned away and left the building before she could say anything else or see the smile on his lips because how fucking cute was it that she wanted to match a monster like him? They were the worst match in the history of ever. This was going to be a disaster. An epically fun disaster.

A country club with a classy lady in matching outfits.

Dad was going to shit himself laughing.

FIVE

Fuck off, the sign read.

Nox was definitely getting warmer. The chain that stretched across the creek was rusted and old, but the sign hanging from it looked new and had been painted in Torren's handwriting. The winding dirt road continued on the other side of the rushing water, and as Nox eased his truck into the rapids, he realized there was some kind of paved road here, hidden by the waves. His tires only submerged about six inches, and then he coasted across the little channel smoothly.

His truck creaked and bounced up the washed-out road as he wound through the trees. There were evergreens and scraggly brush that had lost all their leaves, leaving this place looking half haunted, half like a fuckin' Christmas card Mom used to send everyone in the trailer parks back home. She hadn't even gotten mad at Nox and Dad with their tradition of drawing hidden dicks in the scenery pics like a perverted version of Where's Waldo. Dad had called it Where's Dildo. Mom was used to them misbehaving, and Dad used to say that everyone looked forward to the Fuller Family Christmas cards for the challenge of trying to find the hidden sausage and meatballs.

Another five minutes of driving, and Nox came to a stop at the entrance of a fancy-as-fuck black asphalt circle drive. There was a scorch mark right in front of his tires that stretched through the woods as far as he could see. He would bet his favorite nut hair that the dragon had eaten ashes in a perfect circle around this place because monsters couldn't curb their instincts to lay claim to territory.

The house in the center of the clearing was an utter shock. This was no trailer park. Vyr was holed up in a gol-dern mansion. God, what a prick. Highfalutin fire breather, just like his dad. Of course he wasn't hiding in a trailer. Snob.

The house was two stories, complete with balconies and candles in each window. In the back, there was a massive pond and was that...was that a swan? It was too cold for swans. Nox was definitely going to eat Vyr's pet. Swans probably tasted like chicken.

Nox scanned the yard, but everything was still. Too still. The hair rising on the back of his neck, he inched forward slowly and parked just before he got to the sprawling portico. There were gargoyles carved into the corners. The urge to vandalize this place was overwhelming. All he needed was about two dozen cans of red spray paint, and he would get this place looking homey in no time. He would draw stupid cartoon dragons everywhere with big googly eyes and tiny sky-lizard dicks. God, he hated dragons. Torren had the worst taste in friends.

Nox pulled the Glock from his shoulder holster, checked that the clip was full, and replaced it with a metal-on-metal *click*. When he had his jacket settled over the weapon, he shoved the truck door open and got out, eyes scanning the clearing, all his senses open. The hair wouldn't lower on the back of his neck, and alarms were ringing. There weren't any sounds here. No little animals in the woods, no late season birds. Even the swan was sitting still in the water, staring at him like that feather-skank knew something he didn't.

A soft sound prickled right on the edge of his senses, and he reacted on instinct, ducked to the side. Pain blasted through his left bicep, and he pulled his gun in one smooth motion. Gritting his teeth against the agony of the arrow sticking out of his arm, he jerked his attention to the direction the arrow was shot. Torren was reloading a crossbow on the roof. Fucker.

He lifted his weapon, aimed to not-kill, unlike that prick gorilla, and fired off two rounds. Torren yelled out, tumbled down the roof, and landed hard on the other side of the house.

"Fuck," Nox muttered, yanking the arrow from his arm. Warmth trickled down his bicep. His jacket was going to hurt his range of motion, so he shrugged out of it as he tossed the arrow to the ground. "A fucking crossbow? You could've killed me!" he yelled, his booming voice echoing against the mountains.

"That was the point, asshole!" Torren yelled right before the telltale smattering of pops that signaled

Torren was going silverback. Double shit.

In a rush, Nox struggled out of his holster. Torren charged around the corner of the house. Nox was in serious trouble because that enormous gorilla's bright green eyes were full of rage and promised death. Shhhheeeyit!

Nox closed his eyes and let the beast grizzly rip out of him. Before the pain of the Change had even subsided, he was charging toward Torren, because there was no backing down. He knew this game. How many times had he fought Torren? How many times had he fought all the dominant males in Damon's Mountains? He needed to if he wanted his animal to stay steady. This was just another fight, and at least Torren was limping on a front arm as he bolted toward Nox on his knuckles.

Neither slowed down, and the force with which they collided nearly knocked the wind out of Nox. Torren slammed a fist against his back just as Nox sank his teeth into the gorilla's shoulder right above the collarbone. Nox was going to kill him this time, or die trying. Fucking Torren, always choosing that asshole dragon over everyone else. Over him! He clawed and ripped with his teeth, ignoring Torren's fists. The gorilla opened up his massive jaws, exposing razor sharp canines just before he sank his teeth into the side of Nox's neck. Who would bleed out first, hmm? That was the question. Nox bit down harder and ripped his head backward, shredding Torren's shoulder.

"Stop." The word had been spoken softly, but it had an awful effect on Nox.

A force he didn't understand ripped him off Torren and slammed him to the ground. And from Torren's collision with the earth, he must've felt it, too.

Nox scrabbled, raking his curved, six-inch claws through the manicured grass and deep into the dirt in an effort to get back to Torren and finish this. His focus was complete, and so was Torren's since the silverback was dragging his body toward Nox, too.

Someone stepped between them casually. Fancy loafers, dress pants, a collared shirt, and a bloody arrow twirling between his fingers, Vyr looked down his nose at Nox like he was a bug.

"I said stop," he said coolly, his eyes churning silver. The pupils there were elongated like a snake's. Snake, snake, snake, Vyr was a fucking snake for pretending to be Nox's alpha. *Fight, Bear! Fight everything!*

But that second order had frozen Nox into place like a statue in the fancy winter rose garden that surrounded the house. He could barely breathe, and every muscle was seizing in his effort to break Vyr's spell on his beast.

Vyr knelt down between them, snake eyes never leaving Nox. "Change back," he murmured.

Nox roared at the pain of his animal breaking into a million pieces. Stars dotted his vision as his bellow turned into a man's scream. It hurt so bad. So bad. Nox curled in on himself and shook like a leaf in the fall, trying to wrap his head around pain like that and wishing it would subside, but Vyr was doing something awful to his insides. Nox was on fire. Every cell was screaming with the burn.

Torren was up and walking away like he didn't hurt at all, but Nox was dying.

"Let me guess. My father sent you," Vyr said in a low voice. "But why?"

Nox wanted to stay quiet so badly. He wanted to just get through the burn in silence, but in a blur, Vyr slammed the arrow back into Nox's arm, into the hole that hadn't even healed yet.

Clenching his teeth, Nox grunted at the new wave of pain. "Because you've been sentenced to shifter prison."

Sweat dripped in Nox's eyes as he looked up at the Red Dragon's furious face. "You're going to the cage for burning that town, asshole. And I'm here to put you in it."

"Hmm," Vyr said nonchalantly. Pretend he didn't care all he wanted, but his eyes narrowed to dangerous little slits and red crept up his neck. "And my father only sent you. To die alone. Why?"

That part had bothered Nox, too. Because he was expendable, that's why. He wouldn't ever say that out loud to the Red Dragon though, so he ripped his gaze away and focused on that stupid swan in the pond. God, he wished Vyr would pull the arrow from him or kill him now. Dragons liked to play with their food.

Torren returned with Nox's Glock, smoothly aimed it down at Nox's face, and gritted his teeth. Blood streamed down his tattooed chest from where Nox had shredded his shoulder. Sweat dripped down his face, and his black hair was sticking up everywhere. Nox laughed. "You look so fucked up right now."

"Yet you're the one about to die!" Torren yelled, steadying the gun and resting his finger on the trigger.

"No," Vyr said in a bored voice.

"But he shot me! Twice!"

"You shot me first!" Nox yelled.

"Oh, my God," Vyr muttered, yanking the arrow from Nox's arm.

"Fuck," Nox uttered, gripping his arm to staunch the pain and the bleeding. "I hate you both so much. Like…I hate everyone, but I hate you two the very most."

"Ooooh my God, how will I ever get over this," Torren said in a stupid, mimicking voice, as he waved the Glock around.

"Give me my gun back."

"Or what?" Torren asked. "Look around, you sniveling drop of chode sweat. You're on the ground, Vyr could literally snap your neck and eat your carcass, and in under thirty seconds, there would be no proof you've even been here. Even if he wasn't here? I have a mostly full clip and, again, you're on the fuckin' ground." Torren winced and gripped his bleeding shoulder, jumped up and down a few times, and yelled, "Shit!" to the woods. "Do you have to fight to kill every time, Nox? Really?"

"Again! You shot me with a bow and arrow, you stupid dick archer."

Vyr snorted. "Dick archer sounds funny. Torren, that's your new nickname."

"Fuck you, Vyr."

A deep rumble sounded from the Red Dragon, and he flicked his silver-eyed attention to Torren. "Careful, Monkey."

Torren's jet-black eyebrows shot to his hairline. "Monkey? You be careful, *Lizard*. I'm here risking shifter prison, helping your fire-breathin' ass hide from your fate. You think Damon's gonna stop with Nox? No! This is the first wave. I mean, sure, he sent in the fuckin' D-Team—"

"Hey," Nox complained, sitting up. He was at least C-Team.

"But next time it'll be more. Maybe he'll send Beaston to track us. Maybe he'll send a whole goddamn crew! Maybe he'll come himself, and then what are we gonna do? You'll go to war with your dad in the sky, and what can I do to protect you? Not a thing. Eat Nox, and let's get onto the next war. Drag out our freedom as long as we can."

"I would taste horrible, just so you know," Nox said. "I'm all gristle, and plus you would choke on my big dick."

"God," Vyr muttered, looking nauseous. But fuck him and fuck Torren, too.

"You gonna run forever? Because Torren's right, you cigar-smoking, wine-drinking, money-monger mother fucker. You aren't any different from anybody else. Money won't get you out of paying for what you did in Covington! You nearly burned that place to the ground, and the humans need to make an example of you. Should've been more careful, Red. Now you have to pay the consequences, same as every other tom, dick, and harry nutsack who screws up an entire town."

"To save the Red Havoc Crew and to save Torren's sister," Vyr said in a calm tone. His snake eyes looked crazy right now, though.

"Oh, please. You pulled out your fire and ate all those gorillas and lions because you don't have any control. You like war too much. One year in shifter prison and then start over." Nox struggled to his feet, not even bothering to cover his dick, because why would he? It was huge and he was proud. He should show it to Nevada. She would fall in love with him and have like a dozen little fox babies that looked like him.

Vyr narrowed his eyes and looked slightly terrifying. "What was that?"

"What was what, you weirdo?"

A slow, feral smile curved Vyr's lips, and he ran a hand through his red hair. "You gotta girl, Ob-Noxious?"

"Don't call me that," he muttered. "And no."

Vyr canted his head and leveled Nox with those mercury-colored reptile eyes. "Fox."

Nox's heart hammered against his sternum. He hadn't mentioned Nevada. Not out loud, and now there was a headache building right behind his eyes. Something was happening. His skull felt like it was burning with that same awful sensation from earlier when Vyr had forced his Change.

"What are you?" Nox asked, leaning back on his folded legs, as far away from Vyr as possible.

Vyr's smile dipped from his face, and his voice went hard as a stone. "I'm a lot of things."

Nox flicked his gaze to Torren, but the silverback shifter didn't look surprised at all by Vyr's terrifying admission. Okay, Clara, Vyr's mother, was a witch. Or something. She could read tarot cards and see things she shouldn't see. Apparently, Clara and Damon had made an out-of-control dragon son who had at least some of Clara's power. Everyone had always been afraid of the quiet Red Dragon because he was a monster when he shifted, but this new information made the blood drain from Nox's face. Everyone thought Dark Kane, the Black Dragon, was the End of Days. Nope. The fuckin' apocalypse was kneeling in front of Nox.

"You've always been a thorn, Nox," Vyr said. "Since we were kids, you picked at people. You acted out. You were a carbon copy of your fucked-up father." Vyr smiled brightly. "I got fun genetics, too. I'm gonna let you live for a while. I'm not even going to threaten to char you to a crisp and eat you if you betray me and turn me into my father, or human law enforcement. No. If you tell a soul where I am, I'm gonna go after...Texas..." He frowned at Nox, and the burning ramped up behind his eyes. The dragon was digging in his head.

Nox squeezed his eyes closed. *Don't think about Nevada.*

"Nevada," Vyr murmured in a silky, rumbling tone.

"She isn't my girl. I barely know her."

"Okay," Vyr said with a shrug and an empty smile. "Out me then, and don't worry about what I do to her."

"I really hate you," Nox murmured with venom in his voice.

"Flattery will get you nowhere with me." Vyr stood and tossed the bloody arrow onto the grass in front of Nox's knees. "A souvenir."

"You mean a reminder?"

"Yep. You want a beer before you leave my mountains?"

"Your mountains? I didn't see any record of you buying land. I checked three months back."

"Poor detective work, Ob-Nox-ious. I bought this place years ago. Beer?"

Nox spat on the ground at Vyr's feet. Fuck no, he wasn't going to drink a beer with the monster who just threatened Nevada.

As he meandered toward the house, Vyr said over

his shoulder, "Have a safe trip back to my father's mountains."

"I can't go back without you, and you know it. Your father will burn me."

"Not our problem," Torren called as he followed the dragon and tossed the Glock onto the grass. "Have a nice life and death."

Chest heaving, body aching, blood running down his chest and arm, Nox watched the twin assholes leave him in the yard.

If he returned without the Red Dragon, Damon would punish him, and Nox knew down to his bones that he was unimportant. Expendable. But if he gave up Vyr, Nevada would pay, and she wasn't expendable. She was good, nice, and pure.

He couldn't go back to Damon's Mountains, but he didn't like Nevada's name on Vyr's death list.

Couldn't go, couldn't stay.

Cursed.

Nox was knee-deep in quicksand, as usual.

SIX

Dear Nevada Marianna Foxburg,

Your presence is requested at the formal welcome dinner for Nox Fuller on the second day of December. Formal attire is recommended. I've included a dress should you need one.

1010 Briar Way

Be there at six o'clock sharp.

Nevada flipped over the card, but it wasn't signed anywhere. "W-who sent this?" she asked the delivery guy who was holding a large box and vase of red roses.

"There's no name on the ticket, sorry," he muttered.

Awkwardly, she took the flowers and box from him, nearly dropped the box, then recovered just barely with the thing smashed against her hip. She offered a toothy smile like a weirdo and stumbled inside. Oh! She turned and followed him a couple steps as he made his way down the walkway from her apartment to the parking lot. "Thank you," she said in a barely audible voice. She was such a chicken.

Frustrated with herself, she set the gifts down in the entryway of her apartment and shoved the door closed. Nevada untied the shiny red ribbon on the white box and lifted the lid. Inside was a black satin dress, and when she looked at the tag, her eyes nearly bugged out of her head. It was the right size and everything. It looked expensive. Who the heck sent her this? She would've thought it was a fox match, but the note had mentioned Nox. Maybe it was from his friends.

Delicately, she fingered the edge of the soft satin. She should go if it was for Nox. It was only fair because he was going to come to dinner tonight. Hmm, surely she didn't have these happy flutters in her stomach at the prospect of seeing him again.

He must've talked about her to his friends. A grin

stretched her lips. That was a good sign. She wondered what he said about her. It must've been nice things if his friends wanted her to come to dinner.

But...

She couldn't go to dinner with strangers. Already, she was fighting a panic attack over eating dinner at the country club with her family, and she'd known them since birth.

But...

Maybe it wouldn't be so bad to meet new people if Nox was there. He was mouthy and protective, and he probably wouldn't mind if she hid behind him the whole night. No one was scarier than the Son of the Cursed Bear. She would be safe. Safe, safe, safe. Her smile stretched bigger. Maybe he liked her. Right? That's what meeting his friends meant. He liked her.

A long, angry honk sounded outside. That would be her brother, Jack, and his mate, Fanny.

Nevada stood and smoothed out the wrinkles from her fitted dress, shoved the letter into her purse, and sighed as she opened the door. Let the nightmare begin.

Jack honked again as she was locking her door, as

if he couldn't tell she was coming. If she was a brave girl, she would've flipped him off like her sisters did when they were annoyed, but Jack and Fanny were mean and would make tonight miserable if she gave them any attitude.

"Finally," Jack said as she slid into the back seat.

"Um, I could've driven myself."

In the passenger's seat, Fanny twisted around to look at Nevada. "Your brother and I wanted to ride with you so we could have some alone time before dinner."

"Okaaay."

"You see, we have invited someone for you to meet. Well, you know him, but he has agreed to consider you for a pairing if you exceed his expectations. What do you say to that?" Fanny always talked to her like she was a child.

Exceed his expectations? "I would have to say polite decline." Because she never met anyone's expectations, much less exceeded them. And also there was Nox.

Fanny continued as if Nevada hadn't spoken. "Darren would be the perfect match for you because he's older and failed to make a pairing—"

"Darren? He's twice my age, and he's made pairings just fine. Three of them. He just didn't keep them."

"He's very well-off, and your life wouldn't be so sad if you had someone to share it with and had babies."

"You and Jack don't have babies."

"Yet. We are in our first year and not rushing because we are so happy where we are. But you could benefit by giving a man offspring and attaching him to you. Make it hard for Darren to leave. His other mates failed to do that, but he's desperate now. He needs heirs."

"You think he would be a good match for me because he's desperate?"

"Well...yes."

A slap. That's what it felt like—a slap. Was Nevada so valueless that she could only be attractive to a man twice her age who was desperate for kits? Did she not matter at all? Only her ability to procreate? Fanny was still talking, but there was a roaring in Nevada's ears and she couldn't breathe. "Stop."

Fanny was now talking about Darren's job and his

fancy house.

"Stop," Nevada pleaded louder. "Please."

"Listen to her, Nevada!" Jack bellowed much too loud for the tiny car. "I'm sick of watching you sit pathetically in the corner at every family event. Everyone is paired up and happy, and then the second you enter the room, you deflate all the fun. It's like you're surrounded by this fog of misery, and you drag everyone's mood down with it."

"It's not misery. It's social anxiety."

"Excuse," Jack said, flicking his fingers. They were almost to the country club, and a big part of her wished she could open the door and escape to walk the rest of the way there. Jack was driving too fast, though.

"Everyone thinks you should pair up with Darren," Jack said. "*Everyone.*"

"I'm bringing someone to dinner tonight," she blurted out. Her cheeks caught fire, but she forced herself to sit up straight in the back seat. "He's very cute and my age and nice to me. And he isn't desperate." Her words tumbled end over end, spilling from her lips before she could chicken out.

"Who?"

"His name is Nox."

"Nox?" Fanny asked, tossing her a disgusted look. "What kind of pedigree could a man named Nox possibly have."

"No pedigree. I don't care about that." She sounded shaky but was sticking up for herself, and she was kind of proud of that. For strength, she pulled the note from Nox's friend out of her purse and clutched it against her stomach. He liked her. He'd told his friends about her.

"Nox the fox," Jack said with a snort. "What unoriginal parents named him?"

Fanny giggled. Jack chuckled. When Fanny laughed harder, Jack followed suit until they were both belly laughing.

Jerks. Nox was a badass name for a badass grizzly shifter from Damon's Mountains, not a wussy fox like Stupid Jack and Stupid Fanny.

"Well, your name means 'butt,' so who should really be laughing?"

Jack slammed on the brakes so hard she lurched forward and hit her forehead on the back of Fanny's seat. He twisted around and grabbed her hair before she even had time to settle back against the seat. He yanked it hard and growled, "Listen here, you ungrateful little bitch. Fanny went to great trouble to find you a pairing. Do you know how many males rejected you just on your name alone? Dozens, but she didn't give up, and she found Darren, and now you're making fun of her name?"

Nevada winced and ducked her gaze. "You're hurting me," she whispered.

Jack released her hair and shoved her head back hard. "Good. Think twice before you try to be clever again, sister. The den hates you. Best you don't make enemies of your family, or where would you be? Marked with shame, without protection, all alone, and rogue. You would be nothing more than dragon food."

Holding the aching side of her head, Nevada shoved her door open and got out.

"Get back in the fucking car!" Jack yelled.

"I'm going to walk," she said meekly, her gaze on the road under her heels. She was trying hard not to cry, but her eyes were burning and tears were threatening to spill to her cheeks.

Jack hit the gas so hard his tires spun out and left her in a trail of burnout smoke as he sped away. She coughed and waved her hand in front of her face, and now her eyes were burning from tears and smog. She should've ignored Jack's calls all week about riding together and just taken her own car. At least it wouldn't be a far walk. She could see the turnoff for the country club from here.

With a frustrated, tiny human growl—because her wussy fox was holed up deep inside of her shaking and whining—she took off her heels, lifted the hem of her dress, and made her way up the road, ignoring the three cars with her family inside that refused to pull over and offer her a ride the rest of the way.

Her head still hurt where Jack had pulled her hair. He'd always done that when they were kids too, when he didn't like something she did or said. He'd never grown out of the bully phase, but really, that was how most of the den acted. Kindness wasn't a popular virtue, and so Nevada was left on the outside from yet another character flaw.

Her feet hurt by the time she made her way up the winding road and past the golf course a half an hour late. Maybe Nox was already here and could be a buffer when Mom and Dad got onto her for her irresponsibility—as they did anytime she was thirty seconds late or more.

But when she made her way inside the grand room where everyone was sitting for dinner, she didn't see Nox. An awful feeling hit her in the gut like a punch. Maybe he'd come and gone, or maybe he was standing her up. That last part felt right.

Mom looked mad from her seat at the biggest table near the wall. She and Dad always sat on the ends of the great table like a king with his queen. Mom waved her over with a curt, two-fingered gesture, then jammed her finger to an empty seat next to Darren. Crud. She wanted to cry again, and one last time, she searched the crowd and the tables, but Nox really wasn't here.

Of course he was standing her up. She was just Nevada—uninteresting, anxious, and submissive. And he was built like a bodybuilder, so handsome and tattooed and funny, and a dominant grizzly bear shifter to boot. He had no problem talking to people, he was seventeen levels out of her league, and everything was lame. How silly she'd been to get her hopes up like this.

Feeling dejected, she made her way to her seat

and sank into it, wishing with everything she had that she could press her back into it hard enough that she could disappear completely for the next three boring hours. She fingered the soft satin of her flowing dress and huffed a humorless laugh. She'd even matched the black fabric to the black and white plaid shirt he'd said he was going to wear. How stupid could she be?

"Hello, Nevada," Darren said from beside her. "You're looking very healthy tonight. Have you lost weight?"

Gross. Someone kicked her under the table, and she yelped. Across from her, Fanny gave her a filthy look and jerked her head toward Darren.

"Um, no, I haven't lost weight."

Darren frowned and leaned toward Fanny. "You said she was working with a trainer."

"She is," said a deep rumbling voice behind her. "A sex trainer. She's been wearing me out. You're a vodka girl, right?" Nox asked, setting a pair of shots on the fancy cream and gold table linen next to the wine glasses.

The entire table went silent and froze, probably because Nox was dressed in mid-thigh cut-off shorts, a white T-shirt that read *Bone Ripper* across his tightly puckered nipples, and was he wearing...?

"Are those baseball socks?" she whispered, pointing to his yellow and white knee-high socks.

"Why, yes they are." Nox straightened his spine and placed his hands on his hips. He twisted this way and that like he was stretching his back, but it made his dick bulge against the seam of his shorts. She was pretty sure the head was going to poke out the bottom at any moment. He looked like he'd been in a brawl. Although the left side of his face still sported green half-healed bruising, her attention kept drifting back to his crotch.

"What are you doing here?" Darren asked loudly.

"Currently? Currently, I'm here to eat caviar and snails and try to get into this one's pantaloons." He gave Nevada a sexy-boy wink. "She's playing hard to get, though. Skootch, mother fucker," he said to Darren, flicking his fingers at him. "I need to pull up a chair. Are you using this?" he asked loudly to the table behind them. "No?" he asked when they just stared at him like he had three heads. "Great."

With a screeching sound, he pulled the chair across the wooden floor. The entire room got quiet and turned to stare. He flipped it around and slammed it down beside her too hard, then gracefully and slowly lowered himself down beside her. He was invading Mom's space, and if she hadn't looked like she was about to breathe literal fire on Nox, Nevada would've laughed.

"Um, everyone?" she whispered, tinking her fork against a wine glass. "This is my friend Nox. Nox, this is Darren, Peter, Julia, Juliette, Frank, Toby, my dad, Brutus, Gabriella, Donner, Cassie, Brantly, Sarah, Brie, Tanner, Sawyer, Leslie, Jack, Fanny, and my mom, Darla."

"Your name's Fanny?" Nox asked her sister-in-law. "Like a butt?" He scrunched up his face. "That sucks."

Nevada tried not to giggle, truly she did, but she'd said the same thing earlier, and Fanny looked so mad right now.

"Please tell me you're joking," Mom said, her voice trembling with fury.

"Your face is getting really red," Nox observed. "Not good for the blood pressure. Heart disease is more prevalent in women than you'd think, and it's best if you keep calm and—"

"Shut up," she said, slamming her open hand on

the table. One of the wine glasses fell over, but it didn't break, thank goodness.

Nox reached forward and grabbed a shot, then handed it to Nevada with a wink. "New drinking game. Let's take a shot every time alpha mom loses her shit today."

Stunned, Nevada took the shot from him and then startled when he *tinked* her tiny glass with his. She didn't even want to see her family's angry glares, so she tossed the shot back with Nox, then gestured to her dress. "Um, I tried to match you."

"Next time I'll get you a pair of baseball socks, too." His eyes were such a vivid blue as he gave her a sexy smirk. "My dad told me to wear them for good luck, and he said girls like guys in short shorts, so...you're welcome." He leaned back and checked his crotch. "I think my pecker is gonna play peekaboo at some point, so keep an eye on it so you don't miss the show. Why were you late? It was super boring sitting at the bar watching your family talk about stock markets and hearing about some girl named Candy who slept with half the eligible bachelors. I don't think Peter is your match because he ripped a gnarly fart like four seconds before you sat beside him."

Mom choked on the water she'd been sipping, and Nevada pursed her lips against the loud laugh she really wanted to give. "H-his name is Darren," she corrected him, "and ew."

"Right? I would've waited until at least the fifth date for that kind of grotesque behavior." Nox deepened his voice and said the last two words in a hoity-toity tone, and now Nevada had to put a whole lot of effort into not laughing.

"I can hear you, you know," Darren said. "I'm right here, and I did not…pass gas."

"You look sexy as fuck in that dress," Nox said, his gaze twitching to Nevada's cleavage and back to her eyes.

"R-really?" she stammered through a shy smile.

Nox's blazing eyes dipped to her lips and held before his cheeks swelled with an answering smile that made her stomach do weird flip-flops. Beard and all, he was stunning when he smiled.

"I know you," Darren said with a frown in his voice, "don't I?"

"No one knows me. There's really snails on the menu." Nox pointed to the escargot appetizer. "You wanna share some? It sounds disgusting, but try everything once. We should share all our food so we get to try more."

"You want to share food with me?"

"Woman, I shared my nachos with you yesterday. We're practically married. Do you want the duck or the sea bass or both?"

"Both?"

"Good choice." When a four-string quartet began playing elevator music, Nox leaned back in his chair and looked at the band. "This is my jam."

"Can you go now?" Jack asked rudely.

"Sure. I wanna take this little hottie-with-a-body around the dance floor anyway."

Her sister, Leslie, snorted. "I know you're not talking about Nevada."

Nox gave Leslie the dirtiest look Nevada had ever seen on a man's face. "What's that supposed to mean?"

"There isn't a dance floor," Mom gritted out.

"False, you can make any patch of flooring a dancefloor," Nox said, resting his arm on the back of Nevada's chair and stroking her arm gently with his thumb.

Could he tell she was having trouble breathing?

What Leslie had said embarrassed her.

"Look," Nox said, pointing to the carpet beside mom, "a dance floor. Oh, and over there?" He pointed near the quartet. "Another dance floor. There's like a hundred of them in here. Seriously, *Leslie*, what did you mean by that comment? You don't think Nevada's hot?"

"Do you?" Jack scoffed.

Nox pointed to his short shorts. "Boney McDickerson says yes." As a not-so-quiet aside to Nevada, he said, "Your family's awful. Do you wanna dance?"

"Ummm," she said shyly, looking around. "No one else is dancing."

Nox shrugged a shoulder up to his ear and grinned. "I don't care what other people are doing. I want to touch your waist and hold your hand and move with you. Most of all, I want to get you away from here because you're worked up and uncomfortable. Your family isn't that nice, and my animal wants heads to roll right now. We can take a break, laugh a little, get a drink at the bar, and come right back if you want. I gotta give the beast a break, though."

Okay, all that actually sounded amazing. Nox stood like he could see the agreement in her smile. He bowed magnanimously and offered her his hand like she was a princess. And when she slid her palm against his, he kissed her knuckles gently. It would've been romantic if he wasn't flipping off Jack with his other hand. Or maybe that made it even more romantic; she didn't know about these things.

"Please excuse us," she murmured, her gaze on Nox's muscular legs. "I'm gonna go dance with…my…Nox."

"Nevada, sit down," Dad commanded.

She'd never disobeyed anyone her whole life, but she wanted to dance. And Nox was right. She was really uncomfortable with her family. With the entire den, really. She hadn't realized just how uncomfortable until tonight.

He led her through the tables, winding this way and that until he turned in front of the quartet and pulled her into a smooth waltz.

"Well, this is shocking," she murmured.

"That I can dance? My dad made me learn. He said I needed as many women-gettin' weapons in my arsenal as I could get 'cause I was probably doomed to be single forever without them."

"Why would he say that?"

"Because I'm a lot like him." Nox twirled her easily and brought her back to him, picking right up with the steps they left off on.

"Well, I took dance lessons, too."

"Let me guess, for all those highfalutin fox dances where your parents tried to pair you up with eligible boys your age?"

"Well, it sounds gross when you put it that way."

"Well it *is* gross. Look, that wine has bubbles in it."

"It's champagne," Nevada said through a giggle. "Have you never tried it before?"

"Um no. If wine doesn't come from a box, it's too fancy for me."

"But you said try everything once, and if you're willing to eat snails, you should be willing to drink a sip or two of bubbly wine."

"Fine. Don't tell any of my friends I did this," he muttered, taking two glasses from a passing server. "Just kidding, friends are for losers, I don't have any of those. Bottoms up, Sexypotamus."

Nevada had never giggled so much at a family

dinner before. She sipped hers, but Nox drank his down and made a sour face.

"Speaking of friends," she murmured, putting her arms over his shoulder as he slowed them into a simple side-to-side dance. "I like that you talked to yours about me."

Nox set his empty glass on a passing tray. "What do you mean? I told you I don't have any."

"The dinner invitation. And this dress."

He frowned, and when he slid his hands to her waist and squeezed gently, the butterflies in her stomach moved lower. "What invitation?"

Uh oh. Too late to back out now. She whispered, "The invitation for your formal welcome dinner? 1010 Briar Way. Wednesday at six o'clock?"

Nox's face morphed from an uncertain smile to fury in an instant. A soft rumble rattled up his throat, and his eyes changed to a piercing blue so light they were almost white. Such heaviness came off his skin in waves, Nevada couldn't inhale, and she couldn't meet his eyes anymore. Slowly, she backed away a few feet and clenched her hands in front of her stomach.

"Never go to that address."

The sudden seriousness of his tone woke her fox up just enough to want to run away. "Wh-who is it from?"

Nox's one hand slipped back to her waist, and he cupped her neck with the other. Then he dragged a fingertip down her jawline, hooked a finger under her chin and lifted her gaze to his. He lowered his lips to hers and kissed her like they were the only ones in the room. His beard tickled her face, but he tasted so good, and his lips were so soft as they moved slowly against hers. He slipped his tongue into her mouth just once, and then he eased out of the kiss. She'd asked him a question, but for the life of her, she couldn't think of it now. All she could do was hold onto his wrists and stare up into his soft blue eyes and try to stay upright, because that kiss had been so unexpected from a gruff man like him.

His blond brows lowered slightly though, and he looked troubled.

"What is it?"

"I'm gonna go. I should go. I shouldn't have come here." He looked over at her family's table and then back to her with a troubled expression. Nox released her, eased away, and put painful distance between them. "Stay out of trouble, Nevada," he murmured, but there was real warning in his words.

Before she could tell him to wait, beg him to stay, Nox Fuller spun on his heel, made his way out of the country club, and left Nevada staring after him, completely baffled to what had just happened.

That man had walls a hundred feet tall. He was all jokes, and when he got too serious and showed something real, he bailed.

Nox was a runner, but Nevada was a stayer, stuck for always in Foxburg.

And for the first time in a long time, she didn't want boring. She didn't want to stay in her comfort zone, didn't want to be stagnant anymore.

She no longer wanted to coast through life, but wanted a challenge to push her to be better. And the most interesting challenge had just walked away.

She couldn't follow him because he didn't want her to, but she couldn't face her family for another two hours of them picking at her.

She was stuck.

Couldn't go, couldn't stay.

Trapped.

Nevada stood there feeling like she was knee-deep in quicksand and sinking inch by inch into a flatlined, vanilla life that would swallow her whole.

And suddenly it felt like her chance to escape was walking out the door.

SEVEN

"What the fuuuuuck am I doing here?" Nox slapped his leg with the present wrapped in grocery store bags and the pages of a porno magazine he had bought at a gas station. He shouldn't give this to her. Hell, he shouldn't even be thinking about her, much less stalking her back to her apartment.

But Vyr knew where she lived. Right? He'd sent her that stupid dinner invite, so he had been looking into her, and she shouldn't be unprotected from the Red Dragon's game—whatever it was.

Plus, he'd hated leaving her earlier to the wolves, aka the foxes, aka her snobby family, in the country club. He'd sat in the parking lot like a chump, forcing himself to stay outside by sheer force of will. He wanted to dance with her more, kiss her more. Taste her lips, her neck, her wrist, ankles, inner thighs, pussy. She'd started a fire in him with the needy noise she'd made in her throat when he'd pressed his lips to hers. It was soft, a growl meets a helpless sigh, and he wanted her to do that a hundred times more. Nah, fuck that, he wanted her writhing on his cock, screaming his name.

He hooked a hand onto his hip and hung his head, stared at a crack in the concrete walkway before he gave his attention to the apartment window again. The light was on, and a shadow moved across the room inside. His heart rate kicked up at being this close to her. What the hell was wrong with him? He didn't do bodyguard duty. He wasn't a hero. He didn't do protective. He hurt things. That was his gig—hurting. Why did he suddenly think she would benefit from him being anywhere near her? He was the reason Vyr had an eye on her in the first place.

Stupid magical man-witch-dragon. Wizard-dragon? Whatever, it didn't matter. Vyr was magical, he breathed fire, he was huge and destructive, and he had his attention on Nevada. Nox wanted to rip his oversize lizard-throat out and be done with this.

Human law enforcement would probably give him a medal for putting a dragon down. Too bad Damon wouldn't be so charitable with his actions. He would turn Nox to ashes and then eat him. There wouldn't be a cave deep enough to hide from the blue dragon if Nox hurt his son.

Nox tested himself and tried to walk back to his truck, but a growl rumbled up his throat and his legs locked. And there he stood, like a big, dumb statue, breath freezing in front of his face because it was colder than Vyr's heart out here.

Pissed at how weak he was, he turned and chucked the present like a newspaper delivery boy. It flipped end over end toward her apartment until it flew an inch past Nevada's face and hit the door.

"Aaaah!" Nevada had barely ducked out of the way in time.

"Well, why did you open the door? Watch where I'm throwing that," he groused, crossing his arms over his chest. She kept making him feel something he didn't recognize, and he was getting suspicious that this gritty, churning sensation in his chest was guilt. Gross.

Nevada stooped and picked up the gift. "Is this a

Playboy magazine?" she asked softly, fingering the ripped edge.

"Well, they didn't have any wrapping paper with dicks on it, so I had to improvise."

"Or you could've bought normal wrapping paper?"

"Boring."

Nevada scanned the street behind him. "How did you know where I live?"

"I stalked you. I put a tracker on your car that first night at the grocery store, and I'm not sorry so you might as well not act offended."

Her frown was the cutest fucking thing he'd ever seen, and he wanted to bone her like eight times right now.

"Oh." Nevada gave her attention to unwrapping the present.

Now he really wanted to flee because this was a stupid idea. "It's not a big deal." He cleared his throat. "I got them for ten bucks from the store down the street. It wasn't even out of my way. And I give everyone presents."

"Lie," she called him out, jerking her attention from the pair of yellow and white tube socks that were like his. Her face was comically blank, and his gut twisted.

"See," he muttered. "I told you it was nothing. Have a nice life, Connecticut."

"Have you ever bought a girl a present before?" She asked it so softly the wind almost carried her words away before they reached him. "Nox!" she said louder. "Have you?"

"You sure are brave now. I thought you had social anxiety!"

"Well...I do, but that doesn't seem to make a difference with you."

"Well, why not?"

"Because you have issues, too! You can't judge me so I feel like I can...I dunno...say whatever I want."

"I am perfectly normal."

"Lie."

"I have zero issues."

"'Nother lie."

"And furthermore—"

"Lie," she called, hugging the pair of tube socks to her chest. "I think you pop off a lot when you get uncomfortable. It's so you can push people away."

Whoo, she was making him mad. He wanted to

make her stop calling him out. "And what do you do when you get uncomfortable? Hmm?"

"Hide," she said, the word ringing clear as a bell across the small yard. "I hunch my shoulders and get really quiet, try not to be distracting, try not to draw attention. I try to be invisible. I try to be a mouse."

He didn't like that. This wasn't what he'd meant to happen. Nevada looked hurt, her lips were turned down in a frown, and he'd been the cause of it. Fuck. "You aren't a mouse."

"I'm not a proper fox."

"Bullshit. You are how you're supposed to be. You're just surrounded by people who don't understand your language."

Nevada flinched back, and her delicate, dark eyebrows arched up in shock. "Yeah. That's exactly how it feels. How did you know?"

"Because no one understands my language either." And just so she wouldn't pity him, he reminded her, "Which doesn't matter because I hate everyone and I'm happier alone."

She wanted to call out the lie, he could tell. She stood there in that pretty black dress, the hem whipping around her ankles in the wind, her hair lifting off her shoulders, porno-wrapped present clutched to her tits, looking like she was right on the verge of uttering that word again. *Lie.* But she didn't. Instead, she told him, "I eat too many marshmallows, I don't like talking to people, I can't even afford a puppy, or this dress," she said, holding out the fabric of the skirt to the side with her free hand. "A complete stranger sent it to me and I wore it no questions asked because it was this one, or a dress that's two sizes too small that I bought three years ago. And I've worn that dress to all the family dinners for three years and I'm tired of everyone making fun of it. I have to work from home so I don't make people uncomfortable, and I eat all my meals standing up because tables are for families and I'm by myself a lot. And I talk to myself just to hear a voice. Also, I'm good at cooking."

Nox arched his eyebrows, completely unsure of how to respond.

Nevada stomped her foot and huffed a breath like she was frustrated. With him? With herself? Girl brains were terrifying. "Do you want to sit at the table with me and eat leftovers?" she asked suddenly.

"No."

Nevada winced and dropped her gaze as she whispered, "Truth."

"Because I would rather eat your pussy." He was pretty good at wooing girls.

Nevada's eyes got really big. "You do?"

"Well, yeah." He gestured to her perfect cleavage. "Boobs. Butt." He flicked his fingers at her thighs. "You smell like you want me, and it gives me…" He hooked his hands on his hips. This was the point where he was supposed to be polite and normal. "You know…"

"No, I don't know. You've been on a long ride of weird with your answer. Don't stop now."

Nox cleared his throat loudly. She was wearing a dress and had her hair curled so he should woo her into bed properly, the way Mom always said he should talk to girls. "You give me erections. Of my dick." He gestured grandly at his lap. "My dick is erect."

Nevada cracked a smile and let off a giggle. Sounded like a bell. He liked bells.

Now she was blushing, and her cheeks were so pretty that color. She liked when he said nice things, he could tell, so he said, "Your cheeks are the color of vaginas."

"Oh, my gosh," she murmured through her giggling, and now her cheeks were going darker, and he couldn't stop smiling. He was so good at complimenting Nevada.

"You're the worst at compliments," she murmured.

He smiled bigger because he liked when people said rude shit to him. She was good at complimenting him back in his own language. "Thank you."

"You changed out of your short shorts," she said conversationally.

Nox took a few steps closer to her and looked down at his crotch. "Yeah, my balls shriveled because it was so cold. Admission: I wore those shorts to chase you off, but you didn't run."

"I thought they were funny." She lifted the tube socks. "Umm…"

She looked shy as hell right now. God, he wanted to corrupt her.

"I really like this present," she said.

"No!" he blurted out.

"No, what?" she asked, her dark brows knitting into another frown.

"No, I haven't gotten anyone a gift before. Or not like this. I mean, I've given people fish. But mostly I hide them in their trailers."

"Oh," she said, bobbing her head like she understood. "Why do you hide fish in people's trailers?"

"To start a prank war with people I hate less than others."

"You mean people you like?"

"I don't like anyone."

"Okay, who have you given fish to?"

"Torren, like six times. He mostly just got mad so I quit giving him presents. And then we fought a lot. This is the first thing I wrapped up for a girl, though."

Nevada's answering smile looked pleased as punch as she fingered the edge of the Playboy cover. There was a butt-naked girl on there—too skinny for his tastes, though. He liked the way Nevada looked a lot more.

"Darren figured out who you are. And what you are."

Nox snorted. "I care zero percent what that pickle-dick thinks he knows about me."

"He told me in the car that you're registered. He

found you on that government site. He said the den would shun me if they found out I was hanging out with you."

"Why?"

"Because you're from Damon's Mountains, you march to the beat of your own drum, and they fear anything that's different."

When Nox took a few more steps forward, only three squares of cement sidewalk separated them. "You're different."

"Yes," she whispered. "I'm already on the outside of the den, where I'll stay if I don't find a match."

"You mean if you don't say yes to Darren's bullshit business proposal. I heard the way he talks about you. Before you showed up, I was watching your people, trying to figure you out. Darren talked about you like he wanted to rent you."

"He needs heirs."

Rage was a quick boil in his blood, and she was a frightened little critter normally, so he clenched his fists and swallowed the snarl in his throat. "Nevada, if you say yes to that match, you'll be unhappy forever."

"I know." Her bottom lip trembled, and her voice went thick and shaky, too breathy like she was gonna do something horrifying like cry. Oh, God. He should run. He would rather be shot by Torren again than watch the girl he had warm fuzzies deep in his nutsack for go weepy. It made him want to go Red Rage Bear Death on her whole den. "If you cry, know that I'll want to kill Darren, revive him, and then kill him again. And then repeat that process like...eight times. Suck it back in your eyeballs!"

"It's a tear," she said. "It doesn't suck back up." A single drop of water fell to her cheek.

Oh shit, oh shit, oh shit. He closed the distance and patted his hands in the air around her face helplessly. *Go back in!* "What do I do?"

"Probably hug me, and I'll feel better."

In a rush, he crushed her to his chest and froze. "Now what?" he whispered.

"Now nothing," she said in that sweet voice. "Just stay here like this while I tell you my thoughts. And maybe if I get all emotional again, just...pat my back."

In quick succession, he patted her back in hopes of deterring the girl-emotions from rearing their terrifying heads.

"Too rough, and I feel like you're burping a baby. Maybe rub my back. Gently."

When he did, she told him, "Good job." When Nox growled, she corrected herself and said, "Mediocre job." Much better. "I told Darren I didn't want the match, and he said horrible things."

"Oh. That's good. How would you like me to kill him?"

"Nox! You can't just kill everyone."

False. He was really good at killing, but she was a lady and probably wouldn't like that admission so he swallowed it down like a shot and kept rubbing her back in gentle circles because she wasn't crying anymore. If this was all he had to do to stop the tears, he would literally rub her back until he had to take a leak and/or starved to death.

"He told me he is the only one willing to take me because I'm so submissive and not a good fox. He was taking a risk that our kits would have my genetics and be broken like me."

So Nox was probably going to use a knife to disembowel him, or perhaps just run him over with his truck a few times…

"And then he told me no one in the den respects me as a functioning member, and that the sooner I said yes to his proposal, the better it would be for my reputation."

Poison was also an option…

"And then he brought out this stack of papers. It was a contract to pair up, and I read the first two paragraphs and wanted to puke in the front seat of his fancy Lexus because he was trying to make me sign documents that would guarantee I would have at least four kits for him, one after the other, and I couldn't say 'no' any time he wanted to have sex."

Oh, so he wanted a slow death. Head on a spike maybe…

Easing back, she said, "Nox, I told him no. I don't even know how I did that. I never fight anything, but you seem so sure of yourself and brave, and I wanted to be more like that, more like you, so threw the papers in the back of his car. I'm risking getting shunned, and it changes everything. I'll be outside of the protection of the den. I'll be a rogue. Me! I can't even talk to people, and now I'm going to lose my entire support system."

"Your support system sucks big hairy balls, just so you know."

"Well, yeah, but it's all I have."

"You have me."

"Until you leave."

Nox exhaled a gusty breath that tapered into a growl. He didn't like thinking about the leaving her part. Now it wasn't just Vyr who could ruin her life. Darren would keep pushing her into a pairing, and the rest of the den, too. They would threaten and bully her until she got tired and gave in, and then she would actually have to sleep with that crusty old dingleberry. Nox's growl grew louder, vibrating against his chest. Maybe he could kidnap her away to Damon's Mountains and lock her in his trailer like the *Princess and the Pea* and feed her magical beans like *Jack and the Beanstalk*... And what the fuck was he thinking about? Those fairy didn't make sense together, and if he fed her magical beans, they would grow to the sky... Beans were delicious. "Do you like beans?"

She didn't even miss a beat. "I like refried beans in burritos and on chips."

#perfectwoman. And she wasn't even shrugging away from his hug, which definitely involved his boner pressed against her stomach. He was hung like a friggin' horse so it wasn't like she couldn't feel it. She had to know he was ready from the way she was pressing closer against him. Plus, now her eyes were going all soft and drunk-looking, and she was running her hands down his chest and, holy fuck, it felt good when she touched him. Usually, the only touch he received was painful when he was fighting one of the other dominant males back home. That's the only way he'd wanted touch before Nevada.

When she rested her palms against his chest, his body betrayed him completely and his nipples perked up, poking out against his Bone Ripper T-shirt.

Her hands felt so good. Sooo good. But there was this awful, gut-wrenching moment when he knew with certainty that he was going to fuck this up. He didn't know how to do this. Not the sex part. That was easy—stick his dick in her hole, hump, spoog. But with Nevada, it felt like that wouldn't be enough, and he had no idea what that meant. He'd never been this far with a girl, where he actually wanted to make her happy, and not just for now. Not just this moment. He was thinking about her happiness tomorrow, next week, and next year.

"I'm gonna screw this up," he admitted.

Nevada swallowed hard and nodded as though she agreed. But just as a knife was twisting in his gut, she took him by the hand, pulled him inside, and whispered, "I'm gonna screw this up, too."

And that was good enough for him.

EIGHT

Nox Fuller was hot as sin. Nevada would've never in a million years been brave enough to touch him like this—like she wanted—if he wasn't so obviously into her. His hard shaft pressing against her stomach was a dead giveaway. She'd been telling the truth earlier. He was different from anyone she'd ever met. An outsider too, and she wasn't as intimidated because he made her feel safe somehow. Which was insane because just an hour ago, she'd decided to risk being shunned from the den. This was simultaneously the scariest and most exciting moment of her existence.

Her life was going somewhere. Maybe straight to Hell, she didn't know yet, but at least it was moving in a direction instead of standing still.

She led him straight through the living room and hallway and into her bedroom, smiling like a lunatic the whole way. She wasn't even nervous, freaking out, or on the verge of a panic attack at the thought of being close to someone. She was excited instead.

"I live alone," Nox said as she turned at the end of the bed and ran her hand down the hard mounds of his abs.

"Me, too."

"No, I mean I have to live far away from everyone in Damon's Mountains because I want to fight. Because I don't understand people—"

"I don't care about that. I understand it. You don't belong, and I don't belong."

"Yeah, but I have this urge to make you belong."

"What do you mean?"

Nox shocked her and cupped her cheeks gently with strong, calloused hands. "I want you to be okay and steady, and I don't want to ruin you."

"Nox, you can't ruin me."

"I ruin everything. On purpose. I like to. This is the first time I don't want to ruin something, and I don't know what to do."

Oh, this man cared. He really did. He was admitting something hard. Nox the Runner was standing his ground and laying his insecurities in her hands.

"What do you want to do?" she asked.

He looked down at her with those piercing blue eyes, chest rising and falling too fast, his body humming with power as he searched her face. "I want to make you feel good," he said in a low, growly voice.

"Holy moly, yes."

"Say fuck," he whispered, slipping his hands to her waist. He eased her toward the wall instead of the bed. "Say, fuck me, Nox."

Her shoulders hit the sheetrock. "I don't cuss."

"Why?"

"Because...because..." Because Mom had told her it was unbecoming to say cuss words and she would need all the help she could get someday to land a man. It had been ingrained in her head not to say bad words so that maybe a boy would like her enough to keep her someday. And here was Nox, daring her to be bad and give him a filthy word. Here he was, daring her to live a little, change things up. And she liked change lately. At least with him, she did.

"Fuck me, Nox," she said on a shaky, uncertain breath.

He smirked and lifted his chin, looked down his nose at her, his eyes blazing silver. "You made it sound like a question. Maybe we'll play for a while, and then you'll say it again when you mean it."

Tease. Tease! She was ready. She just didn't have confident speech. She parted her lips to argue with him and tell him he was being a brute, but he spun her around, grabbed her hands, and slammed them against the wall. He intertwined their fingers and nipped the back of her neck, then around to the base of her throat as he pressed his body against her back. Slowly, he bent down behind her and lifted the hem of her flowy dress, careful to brush his fingertips lightly along her outer leg as he dragged it up, up her body. And when he had the fabric all rucked up with one clenched fist midway up her stomach, he brushed those fingertips around her hip so softly she shook with chills that trembled up her spine. With anyone else, she would've been self-conscious when he got to her soft stomach, but right as the first tinges of embarrassment surged through her, Nox murmured a curse and told her, "You're so *beautiful*," in a snarly, sexy voice. Big, dominant bear shifter was drawing her fox up. Her inner animal was invisible most of the time, but right now, she was awake, present, watchful. She was ready for something Nevada didn't understand.

There was a soft ripping sound, and then her tattered lacy panties were falling to the ground.

Nox flattened his strong hand against her stomach and then slipped his fingertips down, down, down between her legs. When his fingers touched her wet sex, she let off a moan and arched her back so that her butt pressed harder against his erection.

Nox pushed into her deep, like he couldn't help himself, and the snarl in his throat vibrated through his chest and against her back. His beard tickled her shoulder as he dragged soft, biting kisses from her earlobe down the side of her neck. He was playing with her now, teasing her clit with the tip of his finger, then dipping it shallowly inside of her, up to one knuckle, then back to her clit again. *Oh, my gosh, oh, my gosh*. She wasn't going to last long just from this. She rocked her hips into his touch the next time he pushed his finger inside of her, chasing him, pleading silently.

Another soft growl, and Nox released the fabric of her dress and pulled her hair gently, urging her to bow her back for him, or maybe it was a delicious punishment for pushing his pace. If so, she wanted to misbehave again.

Nevada slid her right fingertips down the wall and then cupped his hand between her legs. In, in, in, she wanted him inside of her.

"Good," he murmured, plucking her earlobe gently with his lips. "Show me what you like. And then I'll show you what I like."

Okay then, hell yes then! Rocking against his hand, she put pressure on his knuckles, and he slid two fingers deep inside of her. God, she just about buckled right there against the wall. Her locked arm wasn't going to support her, so she went to her elbow. Rolling her hips against his hand, she urged him inside again.

"Fuck, you're so ready for me," Nox murmured against her ear as he pushed into her again. "Do you know how hard it is to keep from burying myself in you right now? I want to fuck you so hard and so fast you'll know exactly who you belong to."

His words and his touch were building a fire in

her middle, and when she rolled her hips against his hand faster, he allowed it. She was panting in tiny bursts now, moaning each time he hit her clit just right. This was everything and not enough all at once. And when Nox sucked hard on her neck, hard enough to make a hickey, hard enough to bruise, hard enough to mark her for a day, she lost it. "Nox, Nox," she said mindlessly, begging for more, but unable to put her needs into words.

He pulled her into him tightly, his hard dick pressing against the fabric of their clothes, right against her ass. His fingers were driving deep inside her now, and even though she wanted more of him, she couldn't stop either. Didn't want to. This pressure he was building felt too good, and she was already on the edge of— "Oh! I'm coming, I'm coming." Mindless. She was mindless and boneless, and Nox was holding her up, controlling her body with touch in a way no man ever had.

"Say it," he growled in an inhuman voice.

Her voice steady, and confident, she said, "Fuck me, Nox," just as her orgasm shattered her.

He now was bucking against her back in the same rhythm as he was fingering her, and she was right in the throes of a desperate need that eclipsed anything she'd ever felt before.

"Good," he practically purred against her ear. And then in a wicked tone, he rumbled, "Now it's my turn."

Ecstasy and anticipation swirled inside of her as the jingle of his belt sounded. Yes, yes, to this, she wanted him so badly. With his boot, he kicked her ankles wider, gripped her hip with one hand and shoved the skirts of her dress up her back with the other, and then he pushed the tip of his cock into her by an inch. Big. Nox was just as big as she imagined, but he'd prepared her and she was ready. The next time he slid into her halfway, stretching her, and pulled out slowly as her orgasm pulsed on. The third time? He slammed into her so deep she gasped at the shock of it. Perfect, perfect, this was so perfect. It's like they were made to fit.

Nox bucked into her faster and faster, and when he clamped his teeth on her neck and cupped her sex, her climax began to build again. Again? What was this man doing to her body? She'd barely finished the first one and now with every hard thrust, she was getting closer to the edge of release again. So big, and she was so tight. So good. God, so good. "Harder," she begged as he bit down.

He was so powerful behind her, his abs flexing against her back with every stroke. And right as his snarl turned feral, he grabbed one breast and pulled her against her as he slammed into her deep. His dick throbbed inside of her, and now she was gone too, matching his release. She cried out. And then there were teeth on her skin. Teeth and what should've been awful pain at her neck, but all she could focus on was the pleasure he was giving her. His shaft pulsed on with each stroke until warmth trickled down her legs. But warmth was trickling down her neck too, and for a moment she was confused with the strange sensations overtaking her body. Consuming pleasure and a dull ache and warmth rained down her skin. She smelled blood. The scent of iron tainted the air. He'd bitten her. Hard. Hard enough to make her bleed. But why?

Nox slowed his thrusting, smoothed it out until both of their releases were done and they were twitching with sensitivity.

"You aren't healing," Nox rasped out.

"Foxes don't heal as fast as other shifters," she

whispered, too intimidated to turn around and face him.

He gripped her shoulders and spun her slowly, then pinned her against the wall. He cupped her neck on both sides and searched her face with those feral silver eyes of his, his blond brows drawn down in confusion. "I would say I'm sorry for what I did, but I'm not. I'm not sorry for anything."

"What do you mean? What did you do?" she asked, flinching at a strange pain in her chest.

"I..." His eyes narrowed and his frown deepened. "You know."

"Nooo," she drew out, unease constricting her chest. "What are you talking about? Why did you bite me? Is it some kind of instinct with your bear? Is that something you need to do during sex?"

"Not anymore," he rushed out. "I should go." He knelt and smoothed out her dress until the skirt hung perfectly again. And never once did he look up and meet her eyes.

"Nox?"

"I need to leave, and everything will be okay. It'll be okay, Nevada. I pinky promise." He hooked a pinky around hers and shook it hard once, then did an about face and strode from the room without looking back. He adjusted his pants as he went.

"You're really leaving?" She followed him out to the living room. He was walking fast, and she had to jog to keep up. "I-I don't understand. Did I do something wrong?"

"Don't." Nox yanked open the front door to her apartment. "You're a goddess and I don't deserve you and now I've ruined you, just like I said I would. Never let monsters into your house, Nevada. First rule of survival."

Nox climbed in his truck, and the engine roared to life. His high beams lit up the parking lot, and then he was burning rubber to get out of there. Away from her.

She pressed her hand to the aching bite on her neck and shook her head in utter bafflement. She'd been mistaken. His feelings for her hadn't grown and he wasn't dependable. He was still a leaver and runner.

And now she was without a prospect, soon to be shunned from the den, would be marked and forced out of this territory, and she would probably bear the scar of a bite from a man she'd risked too much for, too soon.

He'd said "first rule of survival," as if he knew what it was like for her, or for her people. The first rule of survival was invisibility for fox shifters.

And what had she done?

She'd let Nox see her—really see her—instead of listening to her instincts to hide.

And now she would bear the scar of that bad decision for the rest of her life.

NINE

Now that he knew what to look for, this place was crawling with shifters. Apparently dens of foxes were huge. Paranoid little non-apex predator shifters knew their place on the food chain and banded together in big numbers in case anyone tried to make waves with them.

His phone rang again for the third time in a row, and Nox glared at the caller ID. Fuckface BlueBalls Dragon. With a growl, he scanned the grocery store parking lot for Nevada's car and parked his truck to wait, just in case she decided on a late-night shopping spree again tonight. It wasn't safe for her until those two creeper tourists moved on through. He'd been watching them, aka stalking them, to see if they needed to be a little deader than he'd left them when they'd messed with Nevada a few days ago. They were apparently here for some big golf tournament at the Foxburg Golf Course, and until it was over and they were far away from here, Nox was going to troll the local grocery store in case his mate needed back up.

Mother fucker! Stop calling her that!

Nox slammed his hand on the steering wheel, pissed at himself. Not because he'd bitten her. Fuck guilt. But because it was torture trying to stay away from her. Two days since he'd left her house with that question on her lips. *Did I do something wrong?*

She was perfect. Classy, beautiful, funny, and easy-going except when she was around people, but he didn't care about that. He didn't like being around people either. She was the type of girl a guy like him dreamed about. That real love, mate-for-life kind of encounter that made him draw up and question everything. His destiny was to be alone, right? He'd been born with too much of Clinton Fuller in him, and he was meant to wander the earth alone, fighting dominants to stay steady, bounty hunting because it was solo work, and wrinkling up year after year until he turned to dust deep in Damon's Mountains. No legacy, no family, no mate, just getting through each day wondering why the fuck he couldn't just be normal like everyone else.

His phone rang again. Stupid Damon.

Irritated, Nox answered, "I don't have any new information for you."

"Where are you?"

"On the road."

"Have you any new leads on Vyr?"

Damon was testing, but Nox knew better than to lie to an ancient. Damon Daye had hundreds of years of lie detection experience.

"What do you know about fox shifters?"

"That they don't exist," Damon said blandly. "Answer my question."

"Vyr doesn't want to be caught." It wasn't a lie, but it wasn't answering the question either. Check-fuckin'-mate.

"Nice try. Do you have any new leads?"

"I met a girl."

Silence greeted him from the other end. Finally, Damon took the bait. "And she's a fox?"

"Yeah."

"Well, you're fucked. Go fall in lust with someone else. Foxes don't give up their own, and they aren't going to let a grizzly into their den. I'm not paying you to stir up a fox den, Nox. I'm paying you to find my son."

"I want to know why."

"That's none of your business."

"See, that's where you're wrong. It's me out here risking my neck to track down your out-of-control fire-breathing dipshit son. There is a ninety percent chance I'm going to be charred and eaten. I should at least know why his own fucking father is trying to send him to shifter prison."

When Damon sighed, it tapered into a prehistoric rumble over the phone that tickled Nox's ear and made him pull the cell away from his face until the noise stopped. God, he hated dragons.

"Have you not seen the news?" Damon asked.

"I hate TV."

"Right. Well, here's the facts. My son burned Covington, which you know, because you broke the line with him. He then ate several gorilla and lion shifters on camera, scorched the earth for twelve straight hours after the battle like he was claiming the Appalachian Mountains, also on camera. He also ate an entire ranch worth of cattle when he finished burning the land. And then he curled himself around a barn and started defending it like it was a castle. When a massive police force was brought in to neutralize him, he blew up four police cars."

Nox snorted. It was kinda funny. If Nox was a dragon, he'd be doing the same kind of destruction. Vyr was a dumbass and Nox still hated him, but at least he was an amusing dumbass.

"All eyes are on the dragons now. There is a lot of heat on Dark Kane, Rowan, Harper, and me. It's even trickled down to Diem. And if that kind of attention stays on us, it stays on our people."

"Eh, that's bad. There is a hundred percent chance of the Gray Backs screwing up."

"Boy, I like how you blame the Gray Backs for bad behavior when your father has been arrested twice this week for spray-painting twelve-foot penises on billboards. They've caused three wrecks because people get distracted—"

"Dick-stracted—"

"This isn't funny!"

"Disagree, and I know which signs he tagged

because I was supposed to do it with him. It was supposed to be our father-son prank of the month, but instead, I'm out here in boring-ville trying not to get eaten alive by your son! Dude!"

"I'm a millennia old, boy. Don't call me dude."

"Dude! Vyr isn't going to skip off to shifter prison because one grizzly shifter, who he hates by the way, told him he should."

"Well, that's what I negotiated, so he has to. One year was better than a lifetime in there. It's better for all of us this way."

"My dad wouldn't put me in shifter prison even if I ate a hundred gorillas. He would've handed me a Tums afterward."

"Well, your father is a delinquent just like you, and he's also not in charge of my mountains with dozens of people depending on him."

"Your parenting skills need improvement. Oh, my God." Nox stared out the window at the flickering neon sign of Essie's Pantry as something hit him like lightning. "That's why you want me to convince Vyr to come in, isn't it? You don't want to be the bad guy to him. You want me to be the bad guy."

"Enough."

"Either way, he's going to hate you."

"I said enough! It's family business, and I've told him a hundred times he has to be careful with the dragon. He doesn't try to control it, and there have to be consequences for his actions. He's a grown man now, and he should have control, but he doesn't. He never even tried. I've told him over and over this would happen, and now I can't protect him like I used to. I can't! He's put shifters everywhere at risk with his behavior, and he has to be punished or the government will make all of our lives a living hell. Find my son, Nox. And leave the foxes alone."

"Oh, the ones you said didn't exist?"

"You have no idea what you're getting into with that. They aren't submissive like they'll convince you they are. Foxes are very clever and very good at staying unseen. They also hunt en masse. You could disappear, and no one would ever know what happened to you. They are the piranhas of our kind, and they are completely silent killers. They govern themselves, and their law is to kill any threat to them, ask questions later. Leave the vixen alone and get to work. You have two days."

The line went dead.

Nox barely resisted the urge to chuck the phone through the front window. Two days and then what? The blue dragon would eat him? But if he tried to take Vyr in, then he was Red Dragon food. Add Nevada and claiming marks and a bone-deep need to keep her safe into the mix, and he was totally stuck. He was like a duck that had fallen asleep on a pond in a snowstorm and woken up to find his feet frozen in the water.

The longer he stayed in Foxburg, the harder it became to leave.

TEN

Okay. She could do this. Nevada was going shopping during the day and would make herself talk to one person while looking them in the eyes. And she would smile and pretend to be a normal, functioning adult.

One person.

Bleh, she wanted to puke. *Just do it. Be the fox, not the chicken.*

Her hand shook as she reached for her apartment door. She hadn't even left her apartment and she was already breaking out in hives all over her face. She would look like she had chicken pox by the time she got to Essie's Pantry. I f she didn't have a full-blown panic attack in the grocery store, it would be nothing short of a miracle.

Determined, she yanked the door open and almost stepped right on a bouquet of what looked like yellow weed flowers. The stems were tied with a pink satin ribbon. Outside, it had started to snow, and there was a thin layer of white all over the yard, but on her welcome mat was a little bundle of springtime.

"They're dandelions," Nox murmured from where he sat against the wall by her door.

He didn't wear a jacket, only a tight black T-shirt with another Bone Ripper logo in white over his left pec. His jeans were worn at the knees, and his black leather boots were scuffed. His blond beard covered most of his expression, but she didn't miss the shadows in his eyes when he'd lifted his attention to her.

No one had ever gotten her flowers before. Nevada stooped, picked them up, and smelled them like she'd seen girls do on romantic television shows. They smelled good and were cold to the touch. "Where did you get dandelions this time of year?"

Nox pushed a scratched, blue cooler forward with the toe of his boot. "My dad shipped them overnight for me. He grows them for my mom all year round in a greenhouse behind their trailer."

"He grows weeds?" she asked softly as she sat down beside Nox and rested her back against the wall. She wished she could lean her head on his shoulder because she was so dang relieved to be near him again. She'd thought he was gone for good, and admittedly, she'd cried last night because the ache in her chest wouldn't go away.

"He used to give them to my mom when they were kids. He would say, 'Look for me in the dandelions.' And when they found each other again when they were older, he gave her them again. He was never good at I love yous." Nox chuckled. "The other kids would give me so much shit because my dad would give me a flower when he was proud of me. I would press them in an old dictionary, and then when they were dry, I would put them in this scrapbook of plastic sleeves. Torren saw it once when he spent the night."

"Torren is your friend?"

"No. I hate everyone."

Nevada frowned and cuddled the flowers to her chest, then scooted close to Nox. "Then why did he spend the night?"

"Because my mom was worried I would end up…" He let the words trail off and swallowed hard as he gave his attention to the falling snow.

"End up, what?"

His lips ticked up in a sad smile. "She was afraid I would end up like this."

The ache in Nevada's chest grew, so she moved closer until their arms brushed. Nox's reaction to her touch wasn't to flinch away like she'd feared. Instead, he lifted his arm over her, rested it on her shoulders, and pulled her tightly against his ribs. And now she got to rest her head on him. He smelled of mint toothpaste, some hot-boy cologne, and the subtle scent of fur.

"She would invite the boys from around Damon's Mountains for sleepovers to try and socialize me. Torren was okay. I hated him the least, but he never understood my language. He is big and dominant and broken like me. He's got animal problems. He'll be sick in the head soon. Totally fucked. He was raised in a small family group of gorilla shifters outside of Damon's Mountains, down in Saratoga. He was an outsider like me. But when he slept over, he saw the sleeves of dried dandelions and asked me why I had a book of flowers. And when I told him it wasn't a book of flowers, that it was a book of I love yous, he laughed. So I beat the shit out of him, and he asked my mom to take him home. She wised up and didn't try to force people to be friends with me after that. Nevada?" he said suddenly, turning to her. His face was so close to hers, his lips only inches away. "I'm not going to be good at it either."

"At what?"

"The I love yous and romantic shit you'll need. I'm not built to be a good mate."

She lifted the dandelions and smiled. "You're doing just fine." Slowly, she wrapped her arms around his waist and rested her cheek on his chest, listening to the quick drumming of his heartbeat. "You don't have to be anything other than what you are with me."

Nox let off a sigh, as if he'd been holding his breath, and his arms tightened slightly around her. He was so strong and steady, all her anxiety melted away. Here, in this little world this feral man had created, she was safe. Not only safe from other people, but safe to unapologetically be herself, and that's what love was...right? It wasn't a trapped feeling. It wasn't a cage. It was freedom. She wouldn't tell him how hard she'd fallen yet because it was too soon, and she didn't want to seem desperate. But her animal had picked him, she'd picked him, and that was that. She would give up her den to have one day like this, where she could breathe easy, feel valuable, and be touched by a man who wanted to touch her because he thought her soul was pretty, not because she could give him kits.

"I did research," she said cheekily.

"Uh oh."

"Yep, I did research on why you bit me, and I found out about claiming marks."

"Woman, you're a shifter. How did you not know about claiming marks?"

"Because foxes don't do those. We stick to our own and don't concern ourselves with what you barbarians are doing. Get it? Bar-bear-ians?"

Nox chuckled and tickled her ribs. Surprised, she wiggled away from his touch and laughed. "I'm not ticklish. Don't even try it."

"Lie," he called her out.

"Well, that's how you're supposed to do it. You pretend early on in a relationship that you aren't ticklish, and then they never try to tickle you again because it's boring if you won't react."

"Yeah, that wouldn't stop me. I'm going to keep tickling you just for the excuse to accidentally touch your boobs. Do you want to fuck?"

"What?" she asked, sure she'd heard him wrong.

"Do you. Want. To fuck?"

"Not romantic."

"We can do it naked this time."

She sighed. "Last time you ran away. It hurt my feelings."

"I will hurt your feelings six hundred times a day because I'm a monster."

"Well try harder not to!"

"I am trying! I hurt other people like eight hundred times a day."

"Oh." Well that was kind of romantic in Nox's way. "I want missionary position."

"Bland."

"That's what I want, and I don't want to call it 'fucking,' and you have to look me in the eyes when you finish. And no more biting."

"I don't have to bite you anymore. You're already mine."

"Hmm. Are you mine?"

"Not yet."

"Doesn't seem fair. I don't want to belong to a man who doesn't belong to me."

Nox blinked slow and slid her a challenging look, his eyes sparking silver. "Then make me yours, little fox."

The smile fell from her face, and her heart hammered against her breast bone. Nox was hot when he went all serious and told her what to do. "And we come at the same time," she whispered, still negotiating.

He gave her a wicked grin just before his lips pressed onto hers. He laved his tongue against hers, once, twice, and then she was in the air, in his arms, being carried into the house. He was squishing her dandelions between them, but that was okay. She was going to press them and dry them and add them to a scrapbook with plastic sleeves. She was going to make her own I love you book. She hadn't missed the meaning of these flowers. He'd had them shipped here just to give to her. He loved her already, as she did him. They didn't have to say it out loud for it to be true.

The door slammed as he kicked it closed behind them, and then she was on her feet again, unsteady but upright as he shoved her jacket off her shoulders and threw it on the ground. He didn't stop stalking her until she was to the couch. The backs of her legs hit the edge of the cushion, and she plopped onto it with a yelp.

"Clumsy," Nox accused through a grin. His crystalline blue eyes danced as he reached down and hooked his fingers in the hem of her jeans. Without even unbuttoning them, he peeled them off, shoes, panties and all, like she was some kind of horny banana.

Daylight streamed in through the thin curtains, illuminating the room. Nox ripped his shirt over his head in one smooth motion and rested a knee between her legs. She could see every line of tattoo ink, every ripple of muscle. This was the part where she was supposed to be self-conscious about her body, right? Well screw that, because Nox was looking down at her with such a hungry expression in his eyes, she couldn't feel like anything but a sexpot vixen right now. Feeling bold, she canted her head and gave him a devilish grin, and then she laid back and spread her knees apart.

"Fuuuuck, woman," Nox murmured, his wide eyes between her legs. "I want to eat that," he said, pointing. Then he jammed a finger at her tits. "Shirt off, I want to fuck those."

"There are rules this time."

"Fuck rules, I break them. Shirt off."

"Missionary, and then you can do whatever you want next time."

Nox gave off a frustrated growl. "I don't know how to do missionary. I've never done it facing forward before."

"What?" Nevada asked in shock, lifting up to her elbow. "Never?"

"Well, no! Animals do it from the back. I'm an animal. You're an animal." He frowned. "This is unnatural."

"This is like a dandelion," she murmured. Did he understand? Did he realize she was telling him another way to show affection for her?

His eyes softened, and he looked so uncertain. It was strange to see that on a big grizzly of a man, shredded with muscles and tattoos and a big manly beard and that long hair on top that flopped in front of his face.

Slowly, Nox lowered himself to her, pressing his weight on top of her until she sank into the couch cushions. Gently, he pulled her sweater over her head, unsnapped her bra in the back, then draped them on the arm of the couch behind her, and as he shucked his pants, his eyes never left hers.

Naked, powerful body humming with tension, he hovered over her. "Nothing scares me but you."

But the way he said it made it sound like not such a bad thing. And plus, she understood. He was creating a tornado of change within Nevada after she had stood still for so long. It was terrifying, but it also felt right.

Lifting up slightly, she pressed her lips to his, and when she relaxed against the couch pillow again, he chased her mouth and stayed with her. His fingertips were gentle as he brushed them through her hair and then gripped the back of her neck. And as his tension eased, he relaxed on top of her, his warm skin blanketing hers until there wasn't an end or beginning to either of them. He felt so good pressed against her, the head of his cock right there at her entrance, teasing. He flexed his abs and rolled his hips forward, pushing all the way into her. He eased back and watched her face when he did it again. Nevada rolled her eyes closed at how good he felt sliding into her and arched her back against the couch cushions just for the chance to be even closer to him. He was filling her just right, touching her just right, and when he brushed his fingertips up her forearm, intertwined his fingers with hers, and pressed her hand over her head against the arm of the couch, the glowing, tingling sensation inside of her heated up even more.

He was being gentle, and sensitive, this man who had probably not lived a gentle day in his life—he was doing it because he cared for her and wanted to meet her needs. And from the awed expression on his face, maybe he'd needed this too, without realizing it.

He leaned down and kissed her lips gently as he pushed into her again. He quickened their pace but kept it smooth, and now the pressure was building fast in her middle. Clawing the nails of her free hand up his flexing back, she bit his bottom lip gently. The soft growl that rumbled up his throat was nothing short of sexy, and his skin under her hand was now covered in goosebumps. He squeezed her hand where he held it above her head and dipped his tongue into her mouth in rhythm with his stroking inside her.

She was so close. Soooo close, and from the way he was speeding up, thrusting instead of easing, Nox seemed close, too.

Nevada wanted to…do something. Something more. Something that would make them even closer. Something that would bind them. It was an instinct, and in her throat a tiny snarl rattled. *Hello, Fox. Where have you been all these years?* Apparently Nox was the only one who could call her out.

Bite.

Nevada kissed down his jaw and then tested him by clamping her teeth gently at the base of his neck. Big, dominant, brawling grizzly let her have his throat. She was shocked. Foxes never gave their throats, but he trusted her.

Bite him.

What, Fox? Bite him? He will bleed. He will hurt.
For a moment, but he won't mind.

So close, the pleasure was blinding.

"Do it," he dared her in a deep, gravelly, inhuman voice. His eyes were silver now. Beautiful brawler. Beautiful loner. Beautiful match.

He bucked into her harder and faster, and she was gone. With the first pulse of ecstasy, she bit down as hard as she could, determined to make it fast for him, and then she released him. He groaned the sexiest sound and covered her lips with his as he slammed into her again. As the first deep throb of his release shot warmth into her, he gripped her hair in the back and locked his eyes on hers like she'd asked.

Her body was floating with the intensity of her orgasm, and his release only spurred hers on, making her body so sensitive. He felt so good filling her up, so good pressed against her, so good with his one hand in her hair, the other pinning her hand above her head.

Nox, Son of the Cursed Bear, the man who thought he was incapable of anything but fucking, had just made love to her.

And as their aftershocks slowly faded away, she leaned up and kissed him in a silent thank you. "Does it hurt?" she whispered, unable to ignore the red streaming down his neck.

The corner of his lips twisted up in a smile. "I think love is the best kind of pain."

With anyone else, that would have been a strange

sentiment. But with Nox, it made perfect sense. He didn't love like other people, and he didn't feel love like other people. He was different from the bones out, and that was more than okay with her. Because she was different from the bones out too, and they could love however they wanted.

"Thank you for the dandelions," she whispered on a breath. "Now I'll always think of you when I see them."

The smile dipped from his face for a moment and was replaced by shock. "You'll look for me in the dandelions?"

Nevada nodded. "I think you should look for me in them, too."

His blond brows furrowed in question. "Say what you mean."

Slowly, she ran her nails up his spine, raising gooseflesh where she touched him. "L-word. Don't run."

The beaming smile on his face was instant, and his eyes were so silver they were almost white. Beautiful beast. He leaned down and kissed her again. It was a steady kind of kiss, one where they just laid there pressed against each other, their mouths soft but unmoving. A tear slipped from the corner of her eye. She'd always thought a beautiful moment like this wasn't made for a girl like her.

Nox eased back with a soft smack of his lips and rested his forehead against hers. "You're terrifying...but I'm not running anymore. Fuck your den, Nevada. They can shun you, but you won't be rogue and you won't be unprotected. I'll take care of you."

There was honesty infused in every syllable he spoke. And utterly stunned by his oath, she cupped his cheek, his rough beard scratchy against her soft palm, and whispered, "Truth."

"I'll do everything in my power to keep you from having to register with the government."

"Truth." Another tear slid from the corner of her eye.

"My body will be between you and anyone who ever tries to hurt you."

"Truth."

"I'll fuck this up."

She laughed thickly. "Also truth."

His voice dipped to a whisper. "But I'll try for you."

She sighed happily and slid her arms around his neck, hugged him tightly. She'd never had a connection with anyone like this. She'd never understood someone so easily. She'd never felt so free to be just as she was.

"Nevada?" he asked, hugging her tight.

"Yeah?"

"L-word."

She smiled up at the ceiling, her eyes burning with happy tears because this was one of those moments a girl dreamed about.

One of those moments where everything changed.

One of those moments where she knew from here on someone would be at her back, and she wouldn't be alone anymore.

L-word. He'd said it with such confidence.

She rubbed her face against his in a sign of complete devotion. And then she whispered, "Truth."

ELEVEN

"What does Bone Ripper mean?" Nevada asked, tracing the logo on Nox's black T-shirt.

He leaned forward and, pulling on his boot, he explained, "It's the name of my company. Bone Ripper Bounty Hunters."

"You own a company?" she said, sitting straight up on the couch.

He chuckled as he laced his boot. "Are you surprised?"

"A little. What does your company do?"

"I'm a bounty hunter. I did all the jobs for the first five years I was in business, but I got too overloaded and had to hire help."

"You're someone's boss?"

"Kind of. I hate talking to the guys I hired. There are three of them who live around the country. I give them the jobs that are closest to them, and they're paid on commission. All shifters. I've got two tigers and a boar. All loaners who work well in this kind of environment."

"What kind of environment?"

"Hunting. Fighting. Not having to deal with people."

Nevada drew her knees up to her chest and wrapped her arms around her legs. "So the people you bounty hunt…they're shifters?"

"Most of them. Or sometimes I get really bad humans. The dangerous ones who ran, or escaped. I like a challenge, and so do the others on my team. If a job's too easy, the hunt isn't as fun, and we get bored."

As he spoke, he kept his profile to her, lacing up his other boot. It wasn't lost on her that he hadn't met her eyes for even a moment while he was explaining, and a little alarm went off in her head.

It was best to ease into serious conversations with a man like Nox. "Do you like it in Damon's Mountains?"

"It's okay. It's a place to stay. I live off in the woods, though. Alone. There's no pros and cons to living there. It's just a place to rest my head between jobs."

"Huh." *Just ask him if he's here bounty hunting one of your people.* "Are you in Foxburg on a job?"

Nox's lips flickered into an empty smile. "You don't even want to know."

Nevada tensed. Uh oh. "Nox, you can't bring one of my people in. They'll be found out, and foxes will be exposed. I'll be exposed."

"It's not a fox hunt, Nevada."

"Foxes are the only ones in Foxburg."

"False statement, and trust me when I tell you, you don't want to know."

"Is this a shut-down? Is this how it'll be? I can't ask about your jobs? Is it dangerous what you do?"

"Yes."

"How dangerous?"

Nox growled and narrowed his eyes at the front door like he wanted to run. He didn't, though. Instead, he turned to face her, pulled the backs of her knees until her legs were bent against his chest, cupped her face, and then uttered, "It's very dangerous, but I'm good at my job and don't take unnecessary risks. I was telling you the truth. You can hear it in my voice. I'm not here to hunt one of your people. I'm hunting something much scarier than anything your den could produce."

"What are you hunting?" she whispered, her blood chilling.

Nox scratched his beard in an agitated gesture and muttered a curse. "The Red Dragon."

Completely stunned, Nevada's mouth plopped open. The Red Dragon? Here in Foxburg? Oh wait, this was Nox. This was a joke. She offered him a slow smile. "Ha, ha. Very funny."

Nox pursed his lips and arched his eyebrows. He definitely wasn't mirroring her smile.

"Wait, are you serious? The Red Dragon?" Panic filled her veins. "You think Vyr is here?"

"I know he is."

"No, no, no! This is Foxburg, population like…zero. There're foxes here, but no dragons. No scary, fire-breathing, people-eating dragons!"

"That invitation you got? That's from Vyr."

Nevada flinched like she'd been slapped. "The Red Dragon sent me an invitation to his lair?" she asked in a squeaky voice.

"Yep." He popped the *p* at the end. "That's why I told you not to go to that address."

"Why does he want dinner with me?" Yep, her voice was an octave too high, and Nox winced at the pitch.

"Because, apparently, he's a fucking magical mind-reading dragon, and he pulled your name out of my head when I tried to bring him in."

"Oh, my gosh. Oh, my gosh! We should call human law enforcement. The army. SWAT. The coast guard, the navy, special forces, the army reserves, the president, and also aliens. If there are aliens out there, we need their help and their technologically-advanced weapons. I saw the video, Nox! Of Covington? He burned everything. He ate people!"

"Well…he ate asshole gorilla shifters and like…two lions."

Nevada waved her hands around in the air. "Wait! Are you defending him? He's evil."

"Woooooould we call him evil?" he asked in a sing-songy voice. "I've seen evil, Nevada. Vyr has an out of control animal, but he's not evil per se."

"I can't hear you sticking up for a man-eater

because I'm too busy Googling video footage that you must not have seen of him tossing a gorilla into the air like a goldfish snack and catching it in his mouth and eating it," she rushed out as she clicked on the video link. Why on God's green and blue planet was this still available to watch?

She shoved the phone at Nox, but he only rolled his eyes. "I know what happened. I was there."

"What?" she yelled.

With a sigh, Nox yanked the phone out of her hand, fast forwarded the video, and then shoved it back at her. "Look familiar?" He jammed a finger at a mass of gorillas and lions brawling with a green-eyed silverback and a...yep, that was a silver-eyed grizzly bear. Horror flooded her. "You were fighting?"

"Well, it was that or the Red Havoc crew was going to be murdered. We weren't just fighting for the hell of it, Nevada. I know that's how the humans spin it—that we were all just mindlessly at war? But that's not actually what happened. The Dunn lions teamed up with not just one family group of gorilla shifters, but all of them. It was a massive pride and the gorillas against one small crew of mostly panther shifters. And some of my people were in there."

"Who?"

"People from Damon's Mountains who didn't do anything wrong. That crew had cubs, Nevada. Torren's sister was in that crew and she— Fuck! What was I supposed to do? Damon called on us all to go help Red Havoc. We were supposed to wait in the woods so the humans wouldn't see the war, but Torren's sister, Genevieve, was being torn to shreds by the lions, and Torren charged before Damon gave the signal. And I don't give a fuck about anyone, Nevada! Before you? I cared for my parents and...fuck! I cared for my parents and for Torren because I'd always wanted to be his friend. He was going to die if he charged in there to save his sister alone. So I went with him. And yeah, Vyr lit up the town. But he helped save Red Havoc. Those cubs have their crew still because we made quick decisions."

Nevada shook her head, completely shocked. "That's not how the story is told at all," she murmured.

"The humans control the press, which is why that video is still available for anyone to see. Because in that video, it shows Vyr as a monster man-eater, not that he's saving a crew. Human law enforcement took all our statements after the battle, and they deemed it self-defense because there was so much proof that the Dunns and gorillas came in to wipe out Red Havoc. But the press still spins the story however they want to. Everyone kept out of shifter prison. Except Vyr, apparently. I'm supposed to bring him in. No humans were hurt, just the assholes who were killing Genevieve's crew. But the Red Dragon will be made an example of."

"And he's hiding out here?"

Nox dipped his chin to his chest once.

"Geez. Why you? Why are you supposed to bring him in?"

"Because I'm good at my job, but I'm also expendable to Damon Daye."

"Fuck that!" she cried, uncaring about her foul mouth. "You aren't expendable to me!" She wanted to cry she was so angry. "Tell Damon no. Tell him you don't want to do this."

"I tried. Damon's not a man you say no to. He'll eat me with no regrets if I push him. He's already pissed that we didn't wait for the signal in Covington. I think he blames me and Torren for Vyr being in the position he's in. If we wouldn't have broken that line and charged the fight? Vyr would've stayed human behind the trees. There would be no video of him going bitey bitey chomp chomp on everyone. Vyr and Torren are friends though, and he wasn't going to let anything happen to Torren, or to Genevieve. And by the way, just because I'm explaining his actions, doesn't mean I still don't fucking hate him. Dragons are all scaly fire dicks. Can't be trusted. I won't miss him when he's in shifter prison."

"Lie," she called him out.

Nox made an angry tick sound behind his teeth and pushed up off the couch. "I don't want to talk about this anymore."

"Because you care about them."

"I don't care about anyone but you."

"And your parents. And Torren. And Vyr."

"Fuck Vyr," Nox snarled as he strode for the door.

"You're running, and you said you wouldn't do that."

Nox slapped the side of his head and rounded on her. He stood there like a bull getting ready to destroy a china shop, eyes the color of churning mercury. "You know how many times I tried to be friends with those assholes? Huh? It was always

Torren and Vyr, and fuck everyone else. Fuck me!"

"Why them? Why did you choose them to be friends with?"

"Because they're just as fucked up as me! I could've felt…"

"Could've felt what?"

"Normal! Okay? I could've felt normal if I could've just made one or two stupid friends. But I couldn't. They had each other, and I'm just the asshole hermit shifter in Damon's Mountains who can't connect with anyone. Who can't stop fighting other males. The crazy one. The cursed one. The one who screws everything up!"

"Because you speak a different language, remember?"

"Fuck languages. I never adapted." Nox's shoulders sagged, and he rested his back against the door. In a softer voice, he repeated, "I never adapted. And now I have to bring Vyr in, and Torren will hate me even more." His eyes went vacant as he stared at something over her head. "Everything's fine."

He was throwing his real feelings away. With those last two words and the forced, empty smile on his face as he opened the door, he was throwing away his feelings because he didn't like to show what he perceived as weakness. Even with her.

As the door clicked closed, her heart broke for him. Her chest physically ached. He'd picked his friends as a child and had watched them from a distance because he couldn't figure out a way to fit into their lives.

There was chronic tragedy in that.

TWELVE

Nox was so angry.

So full of rage.

Fury.

Blood boiling like water on a stove.

Like lava was blazing through his veins.

Not at Nevada, never at her.

She should be able to say what she wanted, and she *saw* him.

Maybe she saw too much, he didn't know. Letting anyone in was fucking terrifying, and now she was dredging up these feelings of not being enough in his youth, and it was Torren's fault. No…it was Vyr's fault for taking Torren under his ugly, tattered, blood-red wings and shielding him from ever making friends with anyone else. Nox had never stood a chance because of that stupid dragon. His fault. His fault. Fucking Vyr's fault.

Nox slid in behind the wheel and slammed the door beside him so hard the truck rocked.

He needed a fight. Yeah, a fight would settle the beast in his middle. Already the grizzly was snarling in agreement. And the only ones who could match him were the two assholes sitting up in that mansion in the mountains.

Can't think straight, can't think.

Nevada had seen him weak. Weak, weak, weak and it was because of the dragon and the silverback. He needed an outlet so he didn't burn up from the inside out. Dad had struggled with the same his whole life. Looking for outlets to tame the savage animal inside of him. *Thanks for the cursed genetics, Dad.*

He could feel her watching before he saw her. His mate. *Mine. My Nevada.* He slid her a glance from where he sat gripping the wheel in a stranglehold. She stood in the open doorway of her apartment, spine straight, long dark hair whipping in the wind, eyes blazing gold as the snow fell in front of her. She looked like a fucking warrior. "Everything is not okay," she said. The window muffled her voice, but he didn't miss the steel there. "Don't do it."

Oh, she had his ticket punched. *She sees too much, way too much.*

Nox revved his engine and gave her a devil-may-care smile. *Get used to this, Mate.* He wouldn't ask her to be tamed, but he wouldn't be tamed either. The blood on his claiming mark hadn't even dried yet, but it was for the best she saw him for what he really was.

"Nox!" she yelled as he spun out of the parking lot.

He would make it up to her later. Probably. If Vyr didn't eat him. He would give her a hundred dandelions and eat her out, make her scream his name and forget why she was mad, rinse and repeat until she forgave him for what he was about to do.

He sped through town, skidding on patches of ice with each turn. The snow was falling harder. If he hadn't been seeing red right now, maybe this place would have been pretty. Picturesque woods blurred by, and the creek he splashed through had chunks of ice in it already. Snow season was here to stay. Bad weather. He could smell it. Smell the storm. Feel it in the aching shin he'd broken falling off a water tower he'd vandalized as a teen.

Nevada. Nevada. Pretty, perfect, curvy angel. She was good. Good to her soul and back, and he was a mess. He would always be a mess, and now they were bound and he was going to drag her down. Nox couldn't get the look on her face when he left out of his mind. He cleared the last of the trees and skidded to a stop in the manicured yard of Vyr's mansion.

Asshole dragon was waiting for him, sitting on the edge of his roof, one leg dangling down, the other knee bent, resting his arm on that one, staring at him with those dead blue eyes.

As Nox got out of the car, pulling off his shirt as he did because, hell yes, this was going down, Vyr jumped from the second story and landed with no impact. Show-off.

"I could hear you calling me out from two miles away, Ob-Nox-ious," the red-haired fire-breather called as he strode toward him. "You gotta death wish today?"

"I told you to stop calling me that, you micro-dicked lizard."

"What's your problem, man?" Vyr barked out. "I gave you an out. Why the fuck are you still here?"

"Because I can't go back home until you're in the cage where you belong, you motherfucking fuck-fuck!"

"Torren's not here to save your ass this time, Ob-Nox—"

Pop-pop-pop-BOOM! Nox let his beast break his body into a bear before Vyr even got the rest of the insult out.

Claws digging into the earth with the desperation to rip that chode's throat out, Nox barreled toward Vyr. Time slowing with every step, he lunged closer. The dragon shifter skidded to a stop and clenched his fists, a look of pure hatred on his face. His body was vibrating, blurring at the edges, and his face was contorting into something monstrous, but Nox was already too far gone in his rage to stop now.

Cursed with this temper.

Cursed with loneliness.

Cursed with being different. With being unacceptable.

Cursed with this bone-deep instinct to fight.

Cursed to let Nevada down. Fuck. Fuck. Cursed to

let her down.

Vyr arched his neck back and roared a deafening challenge that shook the earth, and a blast of fire shot into the air. He squeezed his eyes closed as if it hurt to spew fire as a human. But when he opened his eyes again, they were silver with elongated pupils. He shot a fireball across the clearing. Behind Nox, there was an explosion that blasted heat against his back.

My truck, my fucking truck. He burned my truck! Kill, kill, kill.

"Don't Change!" Torren bellowed. "Vyr, don't you fucking Change!" He was in gorilla form. Freak shouldn't be able to talk as an animal, but he always could. Damaged. Monster. Just like Nox, but they couldn't see he could've been a good friend. A good ally.

From the corner of his eye, Nox could see the massive silverback charging at him from the woods, but he was too late. Nox was about to shred Vyr before he could Change into the Red Dragon.

Three beasts, one collision, and Nox was gonna survive this. Why? Because he had an anchor. He had a reason to live. He had Nevada.

He finally, finally had someone to come back to.

But first...there had to be pain.

THIRTEEN

She wasn't going to make it in time! Nevada pulled into the clearing just as a redheaded man near the sprawling house blew fire into the sky. No dragon shifter in human form should be able to breathe fire. Horrified, she slammed on the brakes and skidded to a stop. There was a silverback Charging Nox, whose enormous grizzly was at a dead run right for the dragon shifter. Nox was so much bigger than he looked on the video.

Nevada was out of time. She kicked her door open and didn't even put the car in park before she was out. Inside of her, something awful was happening. Her Changes were gentle. They always had been because her fox was docile and always tried for maximum comfort. But right now, she was shredding her way out of Nevada. She yelped as she pitched forward. Her body snapped, burned, and broke in a second of agony so blinding she had to close her eyes and hope she wasn't dying. She landed on all fours, and she was off, completely out of control of her animal for the first time in her life.

Ours. He's ours, and he's going to die!

Vyr shot a fireball directly at Nox's truck, and with the impact of the explosion, the entire thing lifted off the ground and flew backward until it smashed into a tree.

"Don't Change!" the silverback yelled, desperation in his inhuman, gravelly voice. "Vyr, don't you fucking Change!"

Nevada was lightning fast in this body. She might not be able to heal as quickly as other shifters, but foxes could book it, and she was running faster than she ever had in her life. Her paws were barely touching the ground as she bolted for the trio of monsters converging in the middle of the clearing.

Just as Nox reached Vyr, Torren slammed into him from the side, knocking him off his path of destruction. The flurry of violence from the gorilla as he slammed his fists against the bear, and from Nox as he ripped into Torren's arm, was something she would revisit in her nightmares. But for now? She had to stop Vyr from Changing and killing them all. And not just the three of them, but from burning the entire town. Her life didn't matter compared to the hundreds he could hurt if the Red Dragon tore out of him.

What do I do? What do I do! The fox wasn't slowing down, but she couldn't rip into Vyr because it would only anger a monster like him. There would be no stopping the Change if she drew blood. Vyr went to his knees and grunted, his face contorted with pain as he slammed his fists on the ground. He screamed through gritted teeth, every muscle bulging in his body as an awful cracking sound echoed through the clearing. Massive red, tattered wings unfurled from his back, spanning the width of the entire clearing and blanketing them all in shadow.

Oh shoot, oh shoot, oh shoot! She was already to him, couldn't stop now, but that dragon was coming out of him, and there was only one thing she could think of to do.

And it. Was. Disgusting.

Nevada locked her legs against her forward movement, spinning in the snow. And then she lifted her bushy, red tail, positioned her butt on Vyr's closed fist...and peed.

"What the fuck?" Vyr gritted out as the bear and gorilla war raged on under the span of his left wing. He yanked his fist out from under her, and his face lost some of its fire as he stared down at his dripping hand with a look of utter disgust.

In an attempt not to get eaten, Nevada dropped to her belly and rolled over, wagged that big, bushy tail of hers as hard as she could. *Look how cute I am! You don't want to eat me!*

Vyr knelt there frozen, staring at her like she was some mythical Pegasus he just realized really existed. And then slowly, he folded those monstrous wings and pulled them back into his body, face contorted with agony the entire time. He looked delirious with pain as he slammed against the ground and rolled to his back, arching his spine as though his body was on fire. When he placed his dripping fist to his forehead, pee-pee sprinkled into his hair. Vyr yelled and looked horrified as he wiped her piddle drops from his hairline with his clean hand. Not clean anymore!

She kind of wanted to laugh, but mostly wished she could find a hole to hide in from the mortification. She'd just taken a leak on the Red Dragon. *Please God, let this be rock bottom. Don't let life get worse than this.*

"Torren, Nox, Change back!" Vyr snarled out in a terrifying, booming voice that tapered into a dinosaur rumble.

Eek. Play dead. Nevada laid there with her feet in the air, perfectly still with her eyes closed.

Nox and Torren's twin roars of pain filled her head, and both turned into human screams within seconds.

"Oh my God, Nevada!"

"She pissed on me!" Vyr yelled.

Keep playing dead.

"So you killed her?" Nox bellowed. "I'll fucking kill *you*! Slowly. I'm gonna rip your guts through your mouth, you— Get the fuck off me, Torren! Ew, your dick touched me. Nevada!"

Her body was hoisted up. Nox's mouth crashed onto hers, and suddenly her lungs inflated painfully. *Stop that!* She nipped him, and he reared back.

"The fuck?" His lip was bleeding, and his eyes

were bright silver. His beard looked really cute. His hair was mussed on top and his tattoos were really dark and his face was red. He looked hot all worked up and naked. Mmm, nipple piercings. Her thoughts were a hurricane right now, spinning around and around. Wait... he looked hot, but he also looked mad. *I'll fix it.* So she licked his lip and crossed her paws and did her best to give him a foxy-flirt-smile.

His face relaxed with relief and he let off a shaking breath. "Were you playing possum?"

She didn't know what that meant, but his lips were cute when he enunciated poss-um. She leaned up and licked his beard to reward him for being a cutie-patootie.

"Dude, she pissed on my hand. Did no one hear me?" Vyr barked out. "And I touched my face with it!"

Nox snorted, and beside him, the six-foot-two, dark-haired, tatted-up behemoth Torren let off what sounded like an accidental chuckle. "Well, it worked, didn't it? And P. S. Nox, you idiot, you almost got us all busted."

"Uh, that's not the main concern," Vyr yelled. "He could've gotten people killed!"

"You probably wouldn't have killed random

people," Torren said, but there were false notes in his tone.

Vyr got to his feet. His shirt was ripped in shreds from his wings, but at least he didn't have his big dangling dick out like Nox and Torren.

Nox dropped Nevada a split second before Vyr's fist crashed into his jaw. There was no recovery time before Nox was pummeling him back. Torren tried to separate them, but the two giants went to the ground, just...wailing on each other.

"I'm getting my crossbow," Torren muttered, sauntering off in the direction of the house.

What? No! He needed to separate Nox and Vyr before they killed each other or the Red Dragon started coming out again.

Flinching at the pain, Nevada forced her Change back to her human skin. She desperately swiped snow out of the way to grab two fistfuls of dried grass, then covered her boobs and her hoohah with them as best she could.

"Stop it right now!" she screeched.

"Fuck!" Nox yelled, hunching at the pitch of her voice.

"Ha, ha!" Vyr said, right before Nox blasted him in

the face with a closed fist.

The dragon shoved him off so hard Nox landed ten yards away and skidded through the snow.

"I hate you!" he yelled at Vyr, getting back up on his feet.

"Yeah, well I hate you, too."

"Both of you just lied," Nevada said with a smile as she looked between her mate and the Red Dragon. "And whoa, I'm not even scared right now."

Vyr's eyes were round as twin moons and honed in on her chest.

"Don't look at my boobs," she admonished him.

"Yeah, asshole, don't look at her boobs!" Nox pointed to Nevada. "Mine!"

A zinging sound whizzed through the air, and Nox spun so quick he blurred. When he slowed down, he was holding an arrow in his hand. What the heck?

Torren was standing near the house, pulling the string back on a crossbow, reloading another arrow.

"You missed, you robin hood wannabe dipshit!" Nox yelled. And then he chucked the arrow in his hand like a tiny javelin, and a split-second later, Torren yelped and grabbed his arm. Mouth hanging open in shock, he looked down at his shoulder where red was streaming through his fingers. Actually, he was bleeding a lot. Nox had shredded the other side of his body, too.

Nox, himself, was black and blue from Torren's fist, and there was blood in his beard where she'd bitten him. Vyr was wiping the hand she'd peed on in the snow over and over, muttering about how he wanted to barf. Her car was inching slowly past them toward the pond, and Nox's truck was on fire, wrapped around a tree, with black smoke billowing into the air. The wind was cold on her bare skin, and she hugged the clumps of grass tighter to her nether regions.

Nevada cleared her throat. "I'm Nevada Foxburg." She looked from Vyr to Torren and back to Vyr. "It's sort of nice to meet you. I think."

"I would shake your hand, but mine is currently covered in urine," Vyr said. "Torren, stop shooting people. Nox, please stop Nevada Foxburg's car from driving into my pond and hurting my swan."

"I killed your swan," Nox muttered as he stomped off toward her slowly moving vehicle.

"What?" Vyr yelled.

"Just kidding, lizard-breath."

Nevada pursed her lips against the laugh that was bubbling out of her throat. "You guys are a mess."

"Speak for yourself," Vyr said in a strange, emotionless tone as he stood gracefully. He canted his head and narrowed his eyes at her, like he was looking straight through her. A sharp pain behind her eyes made her wince and press her palms to her temples.

Vyr approached, one slow step at a time, eyes drilling into her. "Submissive. No…something more. You panic. You don't like people. No. It's not that you don't like them. You don't like talking to them. You don't like being seen."

"Stop it," she murmured, backing away.

Vyr followed her step-for-step and cocked his head the other way. "How many times did you get put in your place as a kit, Nevada Foxburg? I see hundreds."

"Vyr," Nox called from where he'd stopped her car by the pond. "Cut it out!"

Vyr was stalking her faster now, and she stumbled then righted herself as fast as she could as she backed away.

"And every time you fought an order, your people

cut you down," Vyr said. "Over and over and over until you ended up like this. Scared."

"I'm not scared of you."

Vyr frowned. "No, you aren't. Why?"

"I..." She let the explanation taper off because she didn't really know.

"Why?" he growled out.

"I'm not sure. Maybe it's because you tried not to Change. You were trying to protect the world...from you."

"I'm not safe." He twitched his head toward the gorilla shifter near the house. "He's not safe." He flicked his fingers at her neck at her claiming mark. "The mate you chose? He's not safe."

"But he feels safe to me."

"Who, Nox?" Vyr asked. "Your instincts are completely broken. He's a loose cannon."

"Vyr!" Nox yelled, jogging toward them.

She was getting too close to the burning truck. The heat would blister her skin if he kept backing her up like this.

The snow was falling harder, covering all their footprints in the clearing. She was glad for the white downpour so she didn't feel so naked and vulnerable.

Vyr stopped in his tracks, a look of sheer puzzlement on his face. "I don't understand you."

She dipped her voice to a whisper and looked at the snow on the ground. "You don't understand Nox either. He's good. He just reacts differently than other people. He's different, but different doesn't always mean bad." Nevada locked eyes with Vyr. "Surely you can understand that."

Torren now hung behind Vyr, shifting his weight from side to side, as though his feet were cold from the frozen ground. His attention was on her, though.

"I like you, Nevada Foxburg," Vyr said. "It was disgusting what you did to my hand, but after seeing into your mind, seeing what has happened to you to make you submissive like this, it seems very brave that you tried to stop a dragon from Changing."

"Correction," she said, lowering her eyes to the ground. "I didn't just try. I *did* stop you."

"Look at me."

The weight of his dominance was overpowering now that her adrenaline had run its course. Now, he felt like the monster he was. It was as if she was trying to inhale snow instead of oxygen.

"Nevada," he said softer.

Nox's fingers brushed her hip before he placed himself between her and the dragon. "Back off, Vyr. She doesn't like being crowded."

"It's okay, Nox," she murmured.

He stepped out of her way after only a second of hesitation. Good man, letting her stand strong on her own. Oh, she knew he would go to war for her, but he also had no problem letting her speak for herself.

She forced her gaze to the dragon's silver eyes with those elongated pupils. "What?"

"I know about foxes."

"No one knows about foxes," she argued. "We're secretive."

"You're wrong. My father makes shifters his business. He knows a lot. Maybe he knows everything. I inherited his curiosity about the different cultures, and I know what your den is going to do to you. I've seen your memories. In the country club? The way they reacted to Nox? They'll shun you."

"I know," she whispered, feeling miserable.

"Do you know what happens when they shun a fox from the den?"

Her eyes burned, and her chest hurt just to think about it. "Yes."

"What?" Nox asked, confusion tainting his deep, rumbling voice. "They push her outside of their protection, right?"

Vyr sighed and gave his focus to Nox. "You need to make it right with her people, Nox. You need to keep her from being shunned."

"Why? They're assholes. They don't deserve her anyway. I can keep her protected."

"Because they mark the foxes they shun."

"Mark," Nox repeated in a quiet, lethal tone.

"They're gonna mark up her face. Maybe her body, too. They're gonna make it to where any fox who ever sees her knows to ignore her with one glance."

This was the part she'd dreaded telling him. This was the part she'd agreed to when she'd denied a pairing with Darren.

Horror in his eyes, Nox arched his silver gaze to hers slowly. "I won't let them."

"You can't watch her every second. Foxes are clever, patient hunters. She will never be safe from them."

"Then I'll take her into Damon's Mountains."

"And bring more war? My father won't allow her

there. Not when the media is watching so closely. Everyone has to be perfect right now."

Nox shook his head back and forth slowly. He looked like he wanted to retch. "What do I do? She's my mate. I claimed her. She claimed me back." He gestured to his neck. "She's mine to protect. I can't put her back in that den. If you saw in her mind, you know how they treat her. Those are my choices? Let them scar her on the inside or let them scar her on the outside? Fuck that. No more scars. Those stop right now. Over my goddamn dead body will they hurt her anymore."

"You can't go after a den, Nox. They're a hundred strong, and the quiet kind of lethal. You're in way hotter water than you even realize. You took one of their breeders."

"Breeders?" Nox spat in the snow and hooked his hands on his hips. His profile was terrifying. His face had morphed into a monstrous expression. "She ain't no breeder. Not anymore."

"Then run. Run with her," Torren said, crossing his arms over his tattooed chest. He lifted his chin and looked down his nose at Nox. "Take her away from here, take her somewhere there are no foxes, hide so deep in a hole somewhere they have no chance of ever finding you. It'll be a miserable life, and you'll always be on the run. Trust me on this. Looking over your shoulder all the time? It's going to fuck with both of your animals. They'll become paranoid and unmanageable over time."

"Is that what's happening to you?" Nevada asked.

Vyr and Torren both dipped their chins once in unison.

"You won't be just running from the foxes either," Vyr said. "You'll be running from my father too, because he will be pissed when you don't follow through and bring me in."

"Who says I'm not bringing you in?" Nox asked coolly.

Vyr gave him a venomous smile and tapped his temple twice.

"Dick," Nox muttered. "Stay out of my head."

"Wish I could. It's pretty messed up in there." The dragon gestured to Nevada. "You got lucky to find a girl who doesn't mind damage. Too bad she's a fox. Time to go, love-birds. I need less attention on me, and you two are a train wreck waiting to happen."

Nox huffed an empty laugh and looked at Vyr,

then Torren, and then back to Vyr.

"Just like always, right? Crew of two? Torren and Vyr versus the rest of the world." Nox twitched his head and muttered, "Fuck. Everything's fine." He wrapped his big, strong hand around Nevada's. "Come on. We'll figure this out. You don't have to worry," he said gently, eyes trapping hers. "I promise I'll keep you safe."

She smiled sadly. "Truth." Too bad keeping that promise would put him at great risk.

"See you around," she murmured to Vyr and Torren as Nox led her toward the car. She didn't even try to conceal the lie. She knew what this was. It was goodbye to two men who should've let Nox in. He deserved friendship, and these were perhaps the only two shifters strong enough to be that for him.

Sudden anger whipped through her, and she called out, "He would've been really good at a crew of three. You both should know that."

"We aren't a crew," Vyr called.

But when she turned around to give him a dirty look, both Vyr and Torren stood in eerily similar stances—legs splayed in the snow, arms crossed, twin frowns tracking Nox.

"You should watch that video," she called as Nox tugged her hand and urged her faster toward the car.

"Of what?" Torren asked.

"Of Vyr burning Covington. Watch right at the forty-five second mark. Watch who charged out of the woods right along with you two. Watch who risked himself to have your backs."

Whoo, she got bold when she was mad, but they *should* know Nox's value. If she didn't say it now, she wouldn't ever get the chance to.

"Nevada, it's fine," Nox murmured as he opened the passenger's side of her car for her. "Everything's fine."

But as they coasted silently through the clearing and past Nox's burning truck, everything did not seem fine.

FOURTEEN

A snarl rattled Nox's throat just moments before he lurched up from sleep.

After feeling around in the dark, Nevada slid her hand up his tensed back. His skin was cold. "What's wrong?" she murmured.

Nox sat on the edge of her bed, his back to her, skin blue with the moonlight that filtered through her bedroom window. He scrubbed his hands down his face a few times. In a sleep-soaked voice, he scratched out, "Bad dream, little fox. Nothing more."

"You've been shut down all day. Since we saw Vyr and Torren. Talk to me."

With a sigh, Nox rocked up off the bed and away from her touch. Another shut down. He walked into her bathroom and turned on the light. Another shut down. He went to close the door. Another shut down. He stopped and murmured a curse word then, "Nevada?"

"Yeah?"

"Can you shave my beard for me?"

She sat up and locked one arm under her. "Okay, mister." The covers were tangled around her legs, so she kicked out of them and made her way across the cold wood floors to the bathroom. She was wearing an old T-shirt he'd given her that smelled like him. Like his bear and his cologne. It was one of his black Bone Ripper shirts, and it hung halfway down to her knees.

She leaned against the open doorway and watched him gather a trimmer, a shallow tub of warm water, and a razor and shaving cream. He'd been prepared for this.

"You're tired of your beard?"

"For now. I'm tired of hiding, and I'm tired of scratching up your face when I kiss you. You don't heal fast, and you turn red if I carry on too long with you."

He sat on the floor, leaned up against her bathtub.

"Come here."

His eyes stayed locked on hers as she approached him slowly and straddled his legs. She sat in his lap and cupped his cheeks. "What's going on in that head of yours?"

"I wanna know you. I wanna know what you're giving up to be with me. I wanna know what you're gaining. I wanna know what it was like when you were a kit, who your friends were in school, if you're happy, what food you like, and what your favorite movie is. I want to know everything about you."

"That's a long conversation for one night," she said through a smile.

Nox brushed his knuckles against her cheek. "Good thing we have a lifetime."

Her smile deepened until her ears moved with it. Scary bear with everyone else. Gentle bear with her. "How did I get so lucky?"

Nox chuckled and scratched his bottom lip with his thumbnail, right over the thin scar she'd caused with her nip earlier. "If I've tricked you into thinking you're lucky with me? It's me who's the lucky one."

She giggled and picked up the trimmers, turned them on, and waggled her eyebrows at the buzzing sound. "You ready?"

His smile dipped and disappeared, then came back slowly. "I'm ready for it all." Nox arched his neck back and exposed his throat for her. Brave man, trusting her like this, when she knew without a doubt, he trusted very few people in his life.

Nox rested his hands on her bare outer thighs as she ran the trimmer up his face and cut away the long beard that really had kept his face hidden. She took her time because this was their world. This was their moment, sitting here on the bathroom floor, touching, being affectionate, bonding, caring for each other.

"Favorite childhood memory," he said low.

"That one's easy. Every Monday night, the ice cream truck would come near my house. There was this really nice girl who lived down the road. She was in my class in third grade. She was human. Maria. I would beg my mom to let me have a slumber party, but humans weren't allowed in our house. Too many foxes under one roof, and we would've been busted. But on Monday nights, I would run down our long driveway, and Maria would meet me at the ice cream truck, our moms would talk for a while, and we would run around edge of the woods playing. She was so nice. A sweet soul. She never put me down. She told me I was her best friend, and I would just...*glow*. We would get the same ice cream each week because we liked to match. And sometimes we would plan on what we would wear the next week when Monday rolled around again. I made us these matching hair bows one week, and she was so happy with it. Maria never minded that I was quiet, or soft spoken, or that I couldn't meet her eyes when we played. She was fine with me just the way I was, and at the time, that was a really big deal."

"Mmm," he rumbled, turning his cheek so she could trim at a better angle. "What happened to Maria?"

"She moved away when we were in fifth grade. Her dad got a job in Oklahoma."

"Did you find more friends after that?"

"I think it's hard for people to be friends with someone who has social anxiety if they don't understand it."

"What do you mean?"

"I tried in high school to find someone like Maria. It would be good for a while, but they would get tired of me wanting to stay in. Movie nights got boring, and when they wanted to be in crowds, or talk with other friends, I clammed up. People probably thought I was rude, but it wasn't that. I cared very much. I was just...extremely shy, and didn't know how to talk to people. I never got over it. The anxiety stayed exactly the same. One panic attack, and they would bail, and eventually I got scared of that rejection, so I didn't try anymore. I just tried to make a place in the den."

"But you didn't. You stayed on the outside."

"Not my choice. I used to wish I was normal. That I would just wake up and be more outgoing, not have that heavy, fluttering, awful feeling in my chest when I would be in crowds. That I would be able to stick up for myself with my brothers and sisters and parents and cousins and the rest of the den. Never happened, though."

"Do you want to know a bright side to that?" he asked as she finished trimming his beard short.

"Yes."

"You don't realize how strong they made you. It was a slow build, and I bet you feel weak for not being more assertive, but you're wrong. I see steel in you, little fox."

"Oh, no, not me," she said, her cheeks heating as

she scooped warm water and massaged it onto his short whiskers. "There's no steel in me. Everyone walks on me, and I let them."

"Do you? Because today I watched a fox stop the Red Dragon mid-Change. I watched *you*. Couldn't keep my attention on the fight with Torren because you were charging a mother-fucking dragon, and you didn't slow down at all. Little bat out of hell—"

"Who took a piss on his hand—"

"Who was smart about keeping him steady. Don't sell yourself short with me, Nevada. I see you, and I don't buy it. Be self-deprecating with everyone else. Ain't no room for that between us though unless you're joking. You're a little red-furred, gold-eyed hellion. I'm damn proud of you. And oh, my gah! Your animal is so fuckin' cute. I wanted to cuddle you longer but stupid Vyr punched me. Maybe I deserved it, but still...I was having a moment, and he's not forgiven. Your fur is really soft. Not like mine. Mine's rough. And your eyes are so pretty."

Her cheeks were on fire now with his compliments. He liked the way she looked as a human and in her animal form, and that was pretty special to a girl like her. "Your turn. Favorite childhood memory."

"Okay…once a month, my dad would plan this big father-son prank. One time we broke into this silverback shifter's trailer and nailed all the furniture to the ceiling. Kirk was so pissed he and his mate took a week-long vacation away from us. His mate, Alison, thanked us later though, in secret, because she got to go to Cabo. And another time, there was this shifter who slept like the dead. So on his day off, when he was mid-nap, me and my dad hooked up his trailer and dragged it to a different trailer park and left it. Bash woke up totally confused. I mean, he and my dad went to blows over it, but Dad was always down for a good fight."

"Sounds familiar," Nevada deadpanned.

"But my favorite memories weren't the pranks themselves. It was the tradition we had after."

"What was it?" she asked, as she massaged shaving cream onto his jaw.

"He would always take me out afterward to this gas station restaurant fifteen minutes from Damon's Mountains. They had the best fried burritos, and we would order enough to make us sick…just piles of them, and we would sit there and eat them all and talk and laugh over what we'd just done. Then plan our next one. We did that for as long as I can remember. We do it still."

"Clinton sounds like a really good dad."

Nox smiled. "You researched the Cursed Bear."

"I already knew about the Cursed Bear. I used to wonder what it would be like being raised in Damon's Mountains where everyone is so open about being a shifter. I used to fantasize about how it would be if I didn't have to be so secretive."

"It has cons too, Nevada. We were always at war with someone and had to keep that from human eyes. Our secrets were different from yours, but they were secrets just the same."

"You fought in wars?"

"Too many to count. The shifters in Damon's Mountains were part of the first wave who had to register with the government. It created enemies. There was always some crew, family group, or pride after us for some reason or another. Who knows what the right answer is. Registering like we had to do or staying secret like you had to do. Maybe there is no right answer."

"Will I have to register since I'm your mate?"

"You're supposed to, but rules are for suckers, and I'm not gonna out you as a fox shifter. If it came down to it and we got pushed into registration? I'd claim you as human on the paperwork and dick-punch anyone who questioned it."

She sighed in relief as she swirled the razor in the tub of water. She'd been worried about that actually. "What if I cut you?" she asked, poising the razor against his cheek.

"You bit me earlier, and I gave you zero shit for that. It's not the end of the world if you nick me. Take that pressure off yourself." Nox wiped a finger against his jaw and booped shaving cream onto her nose. "It's just you and me."

Well, that did make her feel better. She giggled as she wiped her face on the sleeve of her shirt, and then she ran the razor down his jaw. She was slow and steady about it, but couldn't stop smiling because Nox kept his gaze glued to her face. He looked so lovey dovey, like a school boy with a crush, and she wondered if she'd ever been this happy a single day in her life. How had she gone this long without Nox to make her feel like she belonged?

For a while, the only sound was the *scrape,*

scrape, scrape of the razor gliding down his face. And as he tilted his head farther back for her to drag the razor down his throat, she asked, "Will you still like me if my face is scarred?"

"Yes," he said without hesitation. He gestured to his torso to the long, raised claw marks that had healed long ago into crisscrossing scars that showed even through his tattoo ink. "You never even noticed mine. You don't have to worry about your face though, Nevada. You're safe."

But she knew better. She knew what was really coming, and at some point, whether it was now or ten years from now, she would be marked by her people. It was the greatest shame for a fox to be shunned, but she would learn to be proud of it, because it would mean she cut herself from a place she didn't belong and found something better. Nox didn't know it, and she wouldn't admit it out loud, but though she was submissive and scared of talking to people, she wasn't a runner. Never had been. And she couldn't live the rest of her life looking over her shoulder. She wanted to spend the rest of her life with a steady gaze, looking right at Nox.

She had plans. And now that he'd told her, with

truth ringing clear as a bell in his voice, that he would still care for her anyway, she was going to get the marking over with and get on with her life—with Nox.

Nox grabbed the hand towel beside him suddenly and wiped the leftover shaving cream from his smooth face. His jaw was chiseled and masculine, his smile lines visible now. He looked so different. Softer. He was beautiful, if that term could be coined for a brawler like Nox Fuller. It was the question in his eyes that held her, though. With a slight frown tugging at his blond eyebrows, he pulled her against his chest and rested his chin on top of her head. And they just sat there like that for minutes or hours or days. She didn't know how long, and she didn't care. All she cared about was Nox's steady heartbeat drumming against her cheek, the way his hands felt as he rubbed gentle circles up and down her spine, his scent. All she cared about was feeling utterly complete right here, all wrapped up in Nox.

"You were the best surprise," he said low. "Now you tell me, what's going on in that head of yours?"

But she couldn't because he wouldn't allow her to do what she was going to do. He would take her away, and they would be on the lam from her destiny for always. She didn't want him to live like that. So instead of explaining why the marks needed to happen, she cuddled closer and gave him a content sigh. "Nothing, Nox. Everything's fine."

FIFTEEN

Nevada couldn't get warm this morning. Her skin had been covered in chills from the moment she woke up. Not even Nox's strong arm around her and his hot-as-coal skin against her back could warm her.

She also couldn't help the soft snarl that kept scratching its way up her throat. It was a miracle she hadn't woken Nox as she readied to go to her childhood home.

Her phone lit up. She'd been a clever fox and put it on silent so it wouldn't alert her mate. It was a message from Mom.

If you do this, you can't ever come back. You understand that, right?

Why do you want me to stay? Nevada typed out.

The answer mattered more than anything. Send.

Because you're a Foxburg. You will be the greatest shame of our family, and we will never live this down. You will unseat our place in this den with your selfishness.

Nevada winced at the pain those words caused in her middle. Selfishness? Mom wasn't very good at being a mom. She never had been. She'd always been missing that tenderness that Nevada had yearned for. It was selfish of her to choose her own mate? To choose someone who didn't make her feel alone and awful about herself? It was selfish to want kits with someone who would give them dandelions and plan prank days into their thirties? It was selfish to want not just a better life but a fulfilling one? She squeezed her eyes tightly closed, loosing twin tears to her cheeks.

That was enough.

That was the final hurt she would allow on her insides from her people.

Not after today.

Today would be the worst of her life. It was going to hurt, not just physically, but emotionally, because the people she'd so desperately wanted to accept her all this time would be the ones scarring her, shunning her.

But tomorrow? She was going to wake up sore and aching for what she lost…but she was going to wake up free to gain so much more.

Nox was freedom, and she was going to fight for him.

She shouldered her purse and looked at his sleeping form once more. God, she hoped he found her pretty after today. She hoped he held onto that ability to see her insides first and outsides second. She was about to go to her knees for a chance at a better life, and he was going to be very important in her learning to stand again.

He didn't know it yet, but Nox was about to become the hero he swore up and down he wasn't.

Dashing her knuckles over her damp cheeks to dry them, she straightened her spine and made her way past all the creaky floorboards and padded outside into the gray dawn light.

Her breath froze in front of her like the steam from a train as she made her way down the snow-caked sidewalk. It had been storming all night, and three inches of the sparkling, white powder was on the ground now. Above her, the clouds churned in discontent—fitting for the day.

She was going to do this, and she was going to be tough about it.

She'd prepared.

Nevada set the bag of first-aid supplies in the passenger's seat and slid in behind the wheel. No one would touch her after this was done. No one would help her, and she wouldn't heal very fast, so it was up to her to take care of herself. Nox couldn't see her until she was mostly healed. She'd reserved a room in a hotel a few towns over for a few nights.

This was rock bottom—knowing she was truly alone right now. But this is what Nevada knew about rock bottom. You go over the edge of that cliff, or maybe you're pushed. And at first, the fall isn't so bad because you can see the water below. You know it'll be over soon, and you'll hit the waves and then break the surface, still alive, still breathing. But when things pile up, suddenly the bottom drops out and turns black, you just keep falling, and it's not that exciting roller-coaster-feel in the pit of your stomach anymore. Its uncertainty and fear of the unknown. It's fear that the fall will never end. And when you do finally see that bottom again, it's covered in jagged rocks, and you scream because it's terrifying. You're falling too fast, and there's no landing softly, no landing on your feet, and this is going to hurt. You curl in on yourself right before impact because there's no way you'll survive. And then...you hit, and it hurts, but you wake up lying on your back and looking up at that cliff you got pushed from. Your body is tired and it aches, but that pain means you're still alive. And it's up to you to get up from that rock bottom and start slowly climbing that wall again to get back where you were.

Or if Nevada was really determined and lucky, maybe she could claw her way to something even better.

Today was rock bottom.

Tomorrow she was going to dig her claws into that cliff face and pull herself up toward where Nox was waiting for her. And Nevada was proud of that. Nox had told her he saw steel in her, and now she believed him. Because she *felt* that steel in her. And the snarl in her throat said her fox felt it, too.

From here on, she was shedding the skin of her past, and she was going to make a future with the man she loved.

The trip to her parent's house was a short one, only fifteen minutes to the old cream-colored Victorian house set outside the city limits just beyond Foxburg. Acres of woods surrounded her childhood home. There wasn't a tire swing in the front tree or handprints in the concrete. The house was pristine, just as it had been every day growing up. She and her siblings hadn't been allowed to let it look "lived in." Mom and Dad needed it spotless at all times for den meetings. They were perfect, after all. The perfect family with perfects kits who would find perfect mates someday and populate the next generation with perfect offspring.

She'd been such a thorn, such an outsider. She almost snorted at how uninviting the house looked. Nox would never settle for pristine. His mess matched hers. If she wanted to draw big rainbow dicks in sidewalk chalk all over their driveway, he wouldn't just allow it, he would laugh and join her. If she wanted to paint their house fuchsia and grow dandelions in the front yard, he would help, and he would water those weeds.

She allowed a smile. One hour and this would be

done. She could be brave for such a short amount of time.

Cars and trucks and SUVs were lined up along both sides of the circle drive. From the look of it, the entire den had shown up for her public shaming. God, foxes were assholes. If she had kits with Nox instead of cubs, she was going to teach them to be kind, generous, and accepting. She was going to do everything different and make sure they knew they were loved, every single day. And she had no doubt in her mind that Nox would do the same. Oh sure, they would likely be little monstrous brawlers if his genetics had anything to say about it, but they would be good inside like their father, too. She would make sure of it.

Her siblings and parents lined up on the wraparound front porch as she got out of her car, each with matching scowls as their gold eyes tracked her progress.

"H-hi, family," she gritted out as she came to a stop in front of the porch stairs.

She wanted to meet their eyes so badly, but couldn't. Someday she would be able to look everyone in the eyes. That was her personal goal, but she was on the first legs of her journey, and she wasn't going to be hard on herself. Not today.

"I knew you were going to be an epic disappointment," Jack said, looking down his nose at her.

Clenching her fists in anger, Nevada snarled up her lip and lifted her gaze to Jack. "Yeah, I'm not here to trade insults. I'm here to cut myself off from the den."

"You're not seeing it correctly," Mom said. Her hair was perfectly coifed, and she wore a plum-colored business suit, as though she'd dressed for the occasion. "You aren't gaining freedom today. You are being punished and shamed."

"I see it differently," Nevada murmured. Her voice shook, but at least she was talking, and that was a tiny victory in itself. "You see shame. I see freedom."

Mom's lip flickered up in a hate-filled snarl, and then she jerked her chin toward the woods where the snow was covered in paw prints and where dozens of red foxes stood waiting between the trees. This was going to hurt. One hour. One hour. *Fuck.* Nox was right, cursing helped, so she repeated it in her head three more times. *Fuck, fuck, fuck.*

"Don't just scar her a little," Mom said. "I want her mauled for her insolence. I want her mauled for risking the entire den's exposure. I want her mauled for turning down matches, refusing to conform, and for stepping out of line her entire life. I want her never to be able to look at herself with pride."

"Mom," Leslie murmured, the first tinges of horror tainting her face.

"Hold your tongue or you'll be next," Mom spat out at Leslie, her eyes flashing the color of pure gold. She lifted her voice. "Let this be an example to any of you who decide to step out of line and betray your people! There will be no leniency!"

Chest heaving, Nevada bit her bottom lip hard to stop her tears from welling up in her eyes. She didn't belong, didn't belong. "You'll have to live with yourselves for what you do today," she called. Damn her voice as it still shook like a leaf. "I hope you have nightmares about what you do. I hope your sins eat you alive. I hope you feel poisoned by the memories of what you'll do to me. But know this. Whatever you do? You aren't really touching my soul. You're nothing, and my life will be happy. I won't think about you." She slid her pissed-off glare to her mom and dared her, "Maul me. I'm still going to be free, and you'll be trapped in this empty, boring life where you're all exactly the same, faceless foxes. Unsympathetic, uncaring, unfeeling, brutal. I'm going to be different, and I'll be happier for it. No matter what you do, you can't take that away from me. Mark me, but hear my words. If you ever come after me again, my mate will fucking murder you, and I won't lift a single paw to help you."

"Language!" Mom demanded.

Nevada lifted her middle finger and finished, "I'll let the Son of the Cursed Bear have you. You think you're cutting me off from the den? Hell no. This is my choice. I'm cutting myself from you. Let's get this over with. I have shit to do." She pulled her sweater over her head as she made her way through the crunching snow toward the foxes in the woods.

When she looked back over her shoulder, her siblings and father were making their way somberly down the stairs and following her, but Mom was gripping the railing, arms locked, eyes blazing, body shaking with fury. Good. She shouldn't feel like she was winning. Something had happened during Nevada's speech. Her voice had become steadier, more growly. It didn't shake anymore. She was meeting their eyes because she believed her words. She was going to be better off without them.

One hour.

Nox, I'm sorry. I'm coming back to you.
Everything's fine. Fine. Fine. Everything's fine.

She was shaking now, from adrenaline and fear. As tough as she wanted to be, this would hurt. And she wasn't going quietly either. Nope. She was going to fight back because she couldn't live with her new, stronger self if she didn't.

Nevada kicked out of her boots one by one and left a trail of clothes behind her, uncaring about the dozens of pairs of eyes that tracked her progress into the woods. *Come on, Fox, we have work to do.*

She pitched forward and gave her body to the snarling animal in her middle. Her fox took off at a sprint, but she wasn't running away. She was leading the others to the exact spot she wanted this to happen. It had been her favorite place as a child. It was a clearing she would sneak to when life was heavy, and she would lie in the grass and count the stars.

It was snowing again, big flurries falling all

around her and settling on her thick coat. Behind her, she could hear the excited yips of the hunting foxes. Hunting her. Bloodthirsty little beasties. Vyr was right about them being lethal. Wild foxes didn't have pack mentality like this, but shifter foxes were a different beast altogether. She ran through the unmarred, fresh snow, her paws crunching in the white stuff. She hoped she could make it to the clearing before they attacked. She could recognize their yipping voices in this form. Leslie, Jack, Mom, Dad, Darren...

There it was. She could see it straight ahead, the clearing where she had spent so much time alone. This would be her last time alone here. It would be her last time alone ever. That thought made her braver, so at the mouth of the clearing, she spun and faced them with her lips curled back to expose her teeth, her front end lowered to the snow. Nevada snarled a challenge. She was ready. *Who's first?*

It was Jack who barreled down on her. Perfect. She could see the sea of foxes converging on her, but at least she could brawl the brother who had pushed her around all these years and made her feel worthless. She ran at him and met him, clashed so hard it nearly knocked the wind out of her, but she didn't back down. Not an inch. She clamped her teeth onto his neck and shook her head as hard as she could to do maximum damage. And then the den fell on her.

Pain.

Pain was everything.

Pain was her whole life in this moment.

She felt ripped to shreds. Like she wasn't even in her skin anymore. Iron filled the air. Red painted the snow. Not only hers since she fought like she never had before, but it was a hundred to one. There was a part of her that grew terrified because her face was hurt, bitten into, but they weren't stopping. *Maul her.* Mom's order rattled around her head like a ghost dragging chains.

Did maul her mean kill her?

She couldn't see the clouds anymore. Couldn't see the sky or the trees. She couldn't see anything but red fur and razor-sharp teeth.

But she could hear. It started as a rattling, soft sound and got louder by the second. The earth shook with something she didn't understand. And then a deafening roar of a grizzly bear shattered the battle sounds of the foxes. It filled the air like a hurricane wind and promised blood, promised death.

A layer of foxes was knocked clean off her with one massive swipe of a paw. Long, curved claws barely missed her belly as Nox blasted her attackers into the woods like they weighed nothing. He was frenzy. He was fury. His hackles were raised, and his massive body was flexed and powerful. He was so fast as he bit and clawed and swiped. He didn't stray far from her when he chased. A few paces, then right back to standing over her. She was frozen in shock. He was really here, really going to war with the den for her.

Her Nox. Hers. Her man might be damaged and a loner, but he had her back. Always. And she had his.

Nevada pushed herself up onto all fours, splayed her legs, and ignored the pain of her muzzle as she bared her teeth at the foxes ducking in and out, testing them for a weak side. Too bad for them there wasn't one. Nox was a monster. Her monster. He didn't back down, didn't back up. He pushed forward, no matter how many teeth touched him.

And when those foxes wised up and attacked at once, covering her and Nox completely, for a moment of terror, Nevada thought they would lose. She thought they would lose this battle, lose each other, lose their future, lose everything.

Right up until the point a big, meaty, shiny black hand squeezed the neck of a fox on top of Nevada and chucked it into a tree. The silverback blasted his fists onto the ground, peeled his lips back over impossibly long canines, and roared.

Holy shit. Torren had come, and that meant...

Nevada jerked her attention to the clearing behind her where a wave of heaviness was crushing her cell by cell. Nox and Torren were brawling, but Vyr was walking slowly toward them, head held high, eyes like silver fire, face contorted with rage. "Stop hurting them," he said in a soft, lethal voice.

Some of the foxes looked uncertain and scattered, but most were too deep in war and bloodlust to realize the danger they were in.

"I said stop!" Vyr yelled. The power of his words formed a crack from his feet that split the earth wide open. Panicked, Nevada scrambled to the side so she wouldn't be swallowed by the break in the ground. Others weren't so lucky. Some foxes fell in.

Nox was on the other side with Torren, but with

one fiery look, he shook off a pair of foxes and bolted for Nevada. He charged and then jumped over the splitting earth. He landed bad, sinking his claws into the edge, half his body in the hole. It was getting wider and wider, and now there was fire. Vyr was lighting this place up. Plumes of black smoke billowed, and trees burned. Foxes were scattering, and Nevada was yipping at Nox. *Pull yourself up, pull yourself up, hurry!*

With a grunt, Nox's massive grizzly pitched upward and gathered Nevada under him just as a stream of fire blistered her skin. It was over quick, but Nox tensed and grunted in pain.

No, no, no!

"Vyr!" Torren growled out in that deep, rough voice of his silverback. "Enough!"

"Hear me!" Vyr yelled. "This isn't your territory anymore. These are my mountains now. Nevada Foxburg is under my protection. Even look at her again, and I'll light your fuckin' den on fire and devour every last one of your ashes. I am The Red Dragon. Bring trouble, and I'll expose every dirty, violent, dark corner of your shifter culture and will make it my personal mission to destroy every fox den from the inside out."

His words rang with such honesty, all Nevada could do was lay under Nox's protective body and watch the Son of the Dragon claim the territory.

And then he did something horrifying. As Torren yelled, "Nooo!" Vyr crouched and leaped into the sky. In an instant, a monstrous dragon with scales as red as fire and wings ripped at the edges like some battle-hardened gargoyle lifted into the air, beating his wings so hard to get airborne the snow was blown away. The hurricane-force wind made Nox and Nevada skid thirty yards into the clearing before they jerked to a stop.

The foxes were on the run, but Vyr didn't seem to care about their surrender. He opened his mouth lined with rows of razor teeth and blasted a stream of fire and lava into the woods.

They should run, but she and Nox just stood there staring at the sky, completely frozen. Torren walked slowly on all fours and stood beside Nox, watched the Red Dragon right along with them. Perhaps their instincts were broken, but they didn't move to escape. The boys were beat, cut, bit, dripping red, and she knew she didn't look any better. Her muzzle hurt so bad her head spun and her eyes watered. Panting and shocked, she leaned against Nox's leg for warmth and strength. His fur was coarse, just like he'd said. Coarse to her soft, just like them. They were different in ways that complimented each other, but similar in ways that mattered—a perfect match.

Silverback, grizzly, and fox...and up there? Up in the sky where all the humans of Foxburg would be able to see? There was the scariest shifter on earth. The big dragon who could breathe fire in his human form, and destroy land. He was a man-eater who could read minds, and who had little control over the dragon.

But Vyr and Torren had come to help her and Nox, and in this moment, she knew these were her people, no matter how broken they were.

Vyr dipped to the earth and scooped ashes, arched his back, pummeled his wings, and lifted into the sky again.

There would be no hiding for them anymore.

The bad boys of Damon's Mountains had just announced their presence in Foxburg in a big, fiery way.

SIXTEEN

Nevada sat in the car trembling. She saw in the rearview mirror her face was pallid, the scars down her left cheek were stark, and her eyes looked petrified. But she'd done it. She'd interviewed for a position at the tiny Foxburg Public Library where she would talk to real people until she would get better control over her social anxiety.

She'd been hired on the spot. She was equal parts elated, horrified, excited, and confused at what the heck she had just done—those feelings swirled inside of her on a constant loop.

Nox was going to be so proud. She kind of wanted to cry, because honestly? She was really proud of herself too, and it was a really good feeling. No more hiding in her house or getting worse each year. From here on, she was going to get on with living.

Her phone rang from the cup holder of her car. She fumbled with it with shaking hands, nearly dropped it, then connected the call in a rush. "Yes?" she asked breathlessly.

"How did it go?" Nox asked.

"I got it."

"Are you serious?" Louder, he repeated, "Nevada are you serious?"

"I got the job, Nox. I got the job and I start next week and I'm so nervous but it'll be good and I'll get settled in and I'm gonna try really hard and I really got it." She broke down on the last part and choked on a sob.

"Steel! I knew you'd get it, you little badass. I knew it! Vyr, she got it. What? Fuck you, man." There was murmuring on the other end, and it didn't sound happy. Nox sighed loudly and muttered, "Vyr wants to talk to you." Static blasted across the phone and then Vyr rumbled out, "Your mate set fire to my fuckin' yard." Eek, he sounded pissed.

"I'll be right over," she murmured, throwing the car into drive.

She hung up and shook her head. All she'd wanted was one night when the guys weren't at each other's throats. They tattled to her like children, and she was always caught in the middle because Torren and Vyr still really didn't understand Nox's language. To her, it was easy to see he acted out with people he cared about, but for Vyr and Torren, they just became immediately angry and shut down. But they kept inviting her and Nox over, so at least they were still trying. Still…Nox setting Vyr's territory on fire? Was he trying to claim it for himself? Vyr wouldn't forgive that. His dragon was too dominant to put up with that. Crap on a stick, now this was sucking all the excitement out of her job offer and deflating her completely.

When she finally pulled into the clearing, she squinted at the billowing smoke that indeed was coming from a good portion of the yard. Nox was standing beside it with the swan in his arms. Mr. Diddles, Nox had named him after they caught him humping a duck statue. He was now Nox's second best friend, next to Nevada, though he still threatened to kill the horny little thing every three hours or so. He wouldn't, though. Probably.

"Nox," she murmured as she got out of her car and made her way to him. "What did you do?"

Vyr and Torren were staring at the burn marks with their arms crossed and their backs to her.

"You said I needed to work on using a language they can understand," Nox said remorselessly. "So I did." He gestured grandly to his artwork.

He'd burned the words *Dear Assholes, will you be my friends?* into the yard with some kind of smelly lighter fluid.

A peel of giggles bubbled up her throat. The lettering was very well done.

"It's not funny," Vyr said, twisting around. Oh, he looked angry.

"It's kind of funny. If you think about it."

"I paid a stupid amount of money to have the landscaping done."

"It's wintertime, you snob," Nox said, stroking Mr. Diddles feathers. "No one cares about your perfect yard if it's covered in snow. I improved it. You're welcome."

"I like it," Torren said, still staring at the writing. "Did you use Baskerville Bold."

Nox beamed. "Why yes, I did. It's my favorite font

for vandalism. It's classic, thank you for noticing."

Torren took a swig of his beer and nodded like he was impressed.

"Put my swan down!" Vyr demanded.

"Don't be pissed because Mr. Diddles likes me more than you."

"His name isn't Mr. Diddles, and I swear to God, if you call him that one more time—"

"You'll what? Burn me?" Nox yanked down the neck of his sweater to expose the burn he'd gotten protecting Nevada from Vyr's fire. "Been there, done that, got the scars. Your dragon sucks. I want to be a crew."

"What?" Vyr asked. "No. We aren't a crew. We're just passing time until I figure out how to avoid shifter prison. Or until human law enforcement comes for us." Vyr frowned. "I don't really know what they're waiting for."

Nox set the swan down and approached Nevada with a smirk on his face. Over the past couple of weeks, he'd grown his beard back, but not as long. Now he was keeping it trimmed, and he looked good. His eyes were always clear and happy now. It made her feel happy, too.

"Hi," she said softly as he wrapped his arms around her.

"You're both gross," Vyr muttered.

"So how do we do this?" Torren asked.

"Do what?" the Red Dragon drawled out, sounding tired.

"Become a crew? Do we like…pledge to you? Do you bite us?"

"Ew. No. I'm no alpha, Torren. I think we can all agree on that one."

Nevada snuggled against Nox's strong chest with a sappy smile. "Disagree. You can control anyone you want. You're alpha as fuck."

"Mmm, I like when you say bad words," Nox murmured against her ear, then plucked gently at her sensitive earlobe.

"We should come up with a name for our crew," Torren said. He was grinning now, like he was having fun pissing Vyr off, too.

"Purple Velociraptors," Nox said immediately. "Purple is Nevada's favorite color, and Velociraptors are cool. I've given this some thought."

Vyr stared at him with his mouth hanging open.

"What?" Nox asked rudely, then flipped him off.

Nevada pursed her lips against the laughter that was clawing its way up her throat.

Torren chugged the rest of his beer and dropped the bottle into the yard like a litter-bug. He turned to them, crossbow resting casually against his shoulder. "It needs to be something badass."

Vyr scoffed and stooped to pick up the bottle. "How about the Crew of a Million Bad Ideas?"

Nox said, "Hmm," and twitched his head like he was impressed, but Torren frowned and said, "Veto."

"What about Sons of Beasts?" Nevada asked softly, wrapping her arms around Nox's waist as he rocked her side to side. She'd missed him all day.

They all got quiet, and stared at her. It was Vyr who responded first. "Huh."

"I'm just saying, this would be a pretty cool crew," Nevada sang. "The Son of the Cursed Bear, the Son of Kong, and the Son of the Dragon? Bad boys of Damon's Mountains, all linking up to wreak havoc."

A soft rumble rattled against her cheek from Nox, and it sounded pleased as punch. "My mate is a thousand times smarter than you two."

"And what about you?" Vyr asked Nevada, seriousness tingeing his words. "Where do you fit into the *Sons* of Beasts Crew?"

"I'm the daughter of no one now. I'm starting over, so the name suits me just fine. You didn't see me before, when I stumbled over words, and couldn't meet anyone's eyes. I still can't talk easy outside of you three. Something about this," she said, gesturing to the four of them, "makes me feel okay. Makes me feel strong. Where do I fit? I'm the one that's gonna keep you three from ending the world. I'll be a secret heroine. I'll pee on you whenever you need it," she promised Vyr. She slid a smile to Torren. "And I'll keep you and Nox from shooting each other." Finally she looked up at Nox. "And you…I'll make you happy and keep you steady, like you do for me."

"Sold," Nox said with the biggest, proudest grin she'd ever seen on him. "Let's pledge or bite, or kick each other's asses or whatever to make this crew. I have things to do and those things include—"

"Please don't say it," Vyr said tiredly.

Nox arched his eyebrow. "Nevada."

Vyr sighed and muttered, "I strongly dislike my life."

Torren cracked his knuckles, looked at Nox, and said, "Yes."

"Yes what, you weirdo? Even I suck less at conversation than—oooooh."

Torren stood straighter, his massive shoulders puffing out. "Yes, I'll be your friend. But you're still a dick, and I still mostly hate you. And we're still gonna fight. A lot."

In an awed voice, Nox whispered, "You do speak my language."

"Fiiine," Vyr muttered. "We're a crew. For now. But I'm not biting you fuckers because you probably taste like cheap beer and bad decisions."

Oh, this crew was a mess. They liked to break rules, had unmanageable animal sides, and a mountain of issues between them. But they were also growing something amazing. Nevada didn't even think the boys realized it, but she could practically see their bonds forming. And Nox, her Nox, was finally finding the friendships he'd always wanted.

Hell was coming for them. That much was for sure and for certain. She didn't know why the humans were waiting to bring Vyr in, or why Damon had stopped pestering Nox to bring his son to the electrified gates of that shifter prison. It was way too quiet, but forming a crew would give them more protection. Sons of Beasts against the world. This was their home base, their stronghold. This crew could take them all straight to Hell in a handbasket, or turn into something great, it was impossible to tell.

But for Nevada, the risk was worth it.

"You're happy," Nox murmured. "I can feel it."

She smiled up at him and leaned into his touch when he brushed the scars on her cheek. The scars that had given her freedom. The scars that had given her Nox and this moment with her crew. Her. Crew. "Tell me the L-word."

Nox's gaze dipped to her lips before he leaned down, sipped her softly, then ran his face against the side of hers, scratching her with his short whiskers. When his mouth was right by her ear, he said, "I fucking love you." She could feel the smile just from the swell of his cheek against hers.

Foul-mouthed man. Damaged, loner, prankster, hot-as-fire, perfectly flawed man.

He was a disaster.

He was a masterpiece.

Nevada bit his neck gently, right over the claiming mark she'd given him. A scar that hadn't meant anything before Nox came into her life, and now meant everything. In a whisper, she said, "I fucking love you, too."

Nox chuckled a deep rumbling sound and cupped her cheeks, eased back to search her eyes. His thumb stroked the scars on her face again. He did that a lot. He worried. "I still hate that you were marked, but I think you look like a warrior. So beautiful. You didn't back down an inch, did you, little fox?" He swallowed hard. "But tell me you're okay."

Her eyes welled with tears, but it wasn't because she was hurt. They were tears of happiness. Before Nox, she'd been alone. She'd believed mean things about herself. She'd questioned her value. She'd found rock bottom. And now, because of him, she was climbing her way back up, and for the first time in her entire life, she was feeling deep joy.

He'd given her friends in Vyr and Torren. Terrifying friends who were monstrous in a war, but who were gentle and protective of her.

He'd given her confidence just from the way he looked at her, and saw her, and constantly pointed out the things he liked about her. Things she hadn't thought about before.

He'd given her a desire to work hard and be a

better version of herself.

He'd given her his body for protection.

He'd given her freedom.

He'd given her a voice.

He'd given her a future she was excited about.

And now he'd given her a crew—the Sons of Beasts.

She belonged. Finally, *finally*...Nevada belonged.

She was better than okay.

With an emotional smile, she rested her forehead against his and let him hear every honest note in her voice as she said exactly how she felt. "Because of you, everything's fine."

SON OF THE CURSED BEAR

Want more of these characters?

Son of the Cursed Bear is the first book in the Sons of Beasts series.

For more of these characters, check out these other books from T. S. Joyce.

Son of Kong
(Sons of Beasts, Book 2)

Son of the Dragon
(Sons of Beasts, Book 3)

This is a spinoff series set in the Damon's Mountains universe. Start with Lumberjack Werebear to enjoy the very beginning of this adventure.

About the Author

T.S. Joyce is devoted to bringing hot shifter romances to readers. Hungry alpha males are her calling card, and the wilder the men, the more she'll make them pour their hearts out. She werebear swears there'll be no swooning heroines in her books. It takes tough-as-nails women to handle her shifters.

She lives in a tiny town, outside of a tiny city, and devotes her life to writing big stories. Foodie, wolf whisperer, ninja, thief of tiny bottles of awesome smelling hotel shampoo, nap connoisseur, movie fanatic, and zombie slayer, and most of this bio is true.

Bear Shifters? Check

Smoldering Alpha Hotness? Double Check

Sexy Scenes? Fasten up your girdles, ladies and gents, it's gonna to be a wild ride.

For more information on T. S. Joyce's work,
visit her website at
www.tsjoyce.com

Made in the USA
Coppell, TX
26 August 2023